Y0-BRD-209

Joanna and Ulysses

Books by May Sarton

POETRY
Encounter in April
Inner Landscape
The Lion and The Rose
The Land of Silence
In Time Like Air
Cloud, Stone, Sun, Vine

NOVELS
The Single Hound
The Bridge of Years
Shadow of a Man
A Shower of Summer Days
Faithful Are The Wounds
The Birth of a Grandfather
The Fur Person
The Small Room
Joanna and Ulysses

NONFICTION
I Knew a Phoenix

Joanna and Ulysses

A TALE BY

MAY SARTON

Illustrated by James J. Spanfeller

W · W · NORTON & COMPANY · INC · New York

COPYRIGHT © 1963 BY MAY SARTON

FIRST EDITION

All Rights Reserved

Published simultaneously in the Dominion of Canada by
George J. McLeod Limited, Toronto

PRINTED IN THE UNITED STATES OF AMERICA
FOR THE PUBLISHERS BY THE VAIL-BALLOU PRESS
1 2 3 4 5 6 7 8 9

Dear Ioanna,

Do you remember the little restaurant near Mycenae where we stopped to drink ouzo and eat fresh tomatoes and goat cheese? There you told me this story, your dark eyes glowing with passion and merriment. It is now translated into American and has, no doubt, suffered a sea change. But I hope you will feel that I have been faithful to its essence.

What I did not tell you, was that I too once fell in love with a donkey, a donkey for whom I could do nothing, who was kept shut up in a dark barn in New Hampshire. So your story had for me a particular resonance.

Gratefully yours
May Sarton

Nelson, New Hampshire
February, 1963

Joanna and Ulysses

CHAPTER 1

Joanna stood in the prow of
the boat that wends its way
with mail and passengers from island to island in the
Aegean sea, and let the wind blow her hair wild. It seemed
hardly believable that she was off on a month's painting
holiday at last, after the years and years of waiting for
this moment, years of war, years of near starvation, years
of such stress and horror that she put them behind her,
and held herself now as if she stood in the prow of the ship
of time, her whole being drinking in the wind.

It had been hot when she embarked at Piraeus, lugging
canvases and easel strapped together as well as her two
suitcases. Her father had objected to the bright blue and
green striped slacks. "Dear girl, must you look like a
gypsy?"

"It's a holiday, Papa! On a holiday one may look like a gypsy!"

The banter covered a difficult moment of parting, for always she carried with her anxiety about her father, who was too old to rally as she had done, her father who had lately become as frail as a blade of grass, and whom she cherished with passionate concern as if she could by the intensity of her caring keep death away. Keep death away. Not look back. For a month she was to give herself to joy, to paint, to think, to feel youth, buried so long, rising up in her like sap into the branches of a battered tree.

Joanna had been under twenty when the war was over, and she was thirty now, but she felt much older. For she had had to become a mother not only to her two brothers, but also to her father when she was fifteen and the tragedy (of which they never spoke) took place. Sometimes Joanna imagined that if her father had been willing to talk about it, it might have helped. Instead, he became a finicky old man, a martinet . . . the two boys had escaped his demands, his neurasthenia, and no longer lived at home, but Joanna herself was a prisoner. This holiday alone, this chance to go off by herself and paint for a month was the first she had ever had, and only now, standing in the prow of the boat, alone and free, she realized how tightly the bow was strung, how great her need to recapture the inner person, the real one. She had sometimes managed to get off on a Saturday to paint, but the results were tight and self-conscious as if she felt her father looking over her shoulder. With all his suffering and the darkness

in which he had wrapped himself, he was a good, a severe
critic, and he did not take her painting seriously. Neither
in fact did Joanna herself: she worked in an office all week,
and kept the house going; she nursed her father slowly
back from the years when he simply lay in bed and refused
to get up, to the point where he did go to his office each
day. Yet somewhere deep down inside her there was a
being who was not the dutiful daughter she had forced
herself to become. She felt she had earned a commitment
to this being, the painter, for although she had no illusions
about the value of what she did, painting could, she felt,
become a way of finding out what she really thought about
things, where she was now, at thirty. She was lifted up on
the expectation of the effort and the joy ahead, a joy so
taut she wished she could cry it aloud like a seagull:
"Listen, sky! Listen, gulls and sea, I am Joanna! Joanna,
the painter!" Oh yes, she had kept her innocence, this
Joanna who was no longer young; she had kept her sense
of herself as a wild creature, a person who could address
God or the sky on a man-to-man basis. Let us say, simply,
that she was a Greek, the tall dark woman, standing in the
prow of the shabby boat, exulting.

She had seen one island after another rise up out of the
cerulean blue sea, first a distant hump, then an escarpment
of rocks, sometimes the blond semi-circle of a beach, and
always the white houses gathered like nests wherever
there was the shelter of a small harbor. Now at last they
were approaching the steepest, the most dramatic harbor
of them all—Santorini. Of course she had chosen Santorini

because it is as inaccessible and remote as a dream.

This island is guarded by the sinister hump of the barren, coal-black volcano, which erupted some years ago and, in the ensuing quake, buried half the village in the sea. The sheer cliff on which the new village stands is really the lip of a crater, looking down on the dangerous Cerberus which guards and threatens it. Already, from her vantage point, Joanna could see the narrow zig-zagging path, twisting up from the cluster of buildings on the quay, to the village itself far away on the height. Here within the deep harbor, the water was magically still, and the whole dramatic scene composed itself in flat planes like a painting. It looked hardly real. But the roar of the anchor grinding down was real enough, and Joanna ran back to collect her luggage, to be ready to disembark into the small boat already close to the ship's ladder.

She was in a sea daze, and the quay seemed to rock slightly as she stood there, bewildered for a moment among the shouts and cries of the donkey drivers already competing for the five or six passengers who had disembarked. She stood there, bewildered, beside her pile of luggage, smiling at the sight of so many donkeys, donkeys of every size, color, each with a different saddle or bright blanket thrown over him, attended by their masters who looked, Joanna thought, like delightful bandits in a child's story.

What made her suddenly notice, far down the quay, another scene, so terrible that at first she turned her eyes away? "I have not come here, all this way, to be wrenched apart again, to be wrenched apart by a donkey," she thought and the thought was a prayer, "Please let me not see what I see." But she did see.

What she saw was an infinitesimal gray donkey, the most miserable animal one could imagine, for his whole belly was an open wound; and on the back of this misery two gypsies were loading an enormous wine cask.

At that second, her daze vanished and she strode past the clamor of reputable donkey-drivers without a glance, her eyes blazing. As she drew closer, she could see the hundreds of flies settling like a black film on the great sores, and, worse, the match-stick legs trembling, trembling, as if they would crack under the preposterous burden just forced upon them.

"Murderers!" The word leapt to her lips but she did not utter it. Instead she looked hard at the two men. One was stooped, a harsh stubble of white beard on his face, an old man breathing heavily from the effort of lifting the cask, for a second leaning against it, so Joanna thought the donkey would crumble there and then. The other man had a hateful look of harsh pleasure in what he was doing. He felt her burning eyes upon him and gave her an uneasy, belligerent glance, then spat.

Joanna forced herself to walk two steps forward, and then said quietly, without taking her eyes from his face, "You are going to kill the donkey."

The old man lifted his head and looked at her with dead eyes.

The young man slouched toward her, and spoke in an angry, whining singsong, "He might last to the top," he said, "We'll work him till he drops, and that's that. Do you think we are rich?" He spat again. "We can't afford to keep a sick animal. If he dies, all right, kaput!"

Joanna flinched before the German word. The memories of cruelty and violence swept over her, cruelty about which one could do nothing; she experienced again the corroding poison of helplessness before violence. She felt suddenly weak, as weak as the donkey. The donkey had no strength, it seemed, even to wag its tail at the flies. It waited, just barely able to stand, its head drooping a little. The patience and suffering of the donkey were awful.

And Joanna, in her weakness, turned away. What could she do, after all? What use to stay and witness an agony for which she could no nothing? It was not her business. Then she heard the whack of a stick, and rage gave her courage. Before she knew what she was doing, she had seized the stick by one end and shouted,

"No! No!"

"Leave me alone. I know what I'm doing!" And Joanna felt the rough stick torn from her hands. The old man was pushing the miserable beast from behind, and slowly, slowly, the match stick legs stumbled a step forward.

"I'll buy it!" Joanna said, beside herself. "I'll give you five hundred drachma!" It was the first sum that came into her head—she had no idea what a donkey cost—but it seemed a lot. It must be enough, quickly, quickly, before the donkey crumpled up and died there before her eyes.

The young man said something in a language that she

did not understand, and the old man stopped pushing, and wiped his face on a dirty rag.

"Five hundred?" the young man mocked her. "Are you crazy?"

"Six hundred?" she murmured, not taking her eyes from his. She was caught now. She was a prisoner of their greed, and her weakness. And they took eight hundred drachma before they lifted the cask off the poor beast, and set it free.

There she was, on the quay, where she had stepped so lightheartedly only half an hour ago, as if it were now enemy country. She stood there, shivering, with a dying donkey at her side, and nowhere to sleep.

"It will be all right," she said, and saw him wince as she laid a hand gently on his forehead, as if he expected a blow. How hot his head was, poor beastie! They stood there a few seconds, leaning together like two orphans, and Joanna looked up at the climb ahead with dismay.

"Come," she said, taking the frayed rope in her hands. The donkey followed at once, before she had given the slightest tug, and this was the first sign between them. He followed her to the pile of luggage. If she strapped the easel and canvases to her back, she could manage to carry the suitcases; hiring a donkey was out of the question now . . . besides they had all left. They were halfway up to the village, laughing and talking. Even the gypsies had disappeared.

"I must be mad," she said to the donkey, who stood there, wrapped in his patience. The immensity of what she had undertaken swept over her in a wave. She sensed that here in this poor village where all lived close to poverty, an act such as hers would seem unpleasant, even indecent. Only the very rich could afford such whims. But the joke was on her, for she was not rich. And the truth was that she felt exhaustion before the effort ahead.

"Well, Ulysses, let's go!" She had found a name for the donkey, without even considering the matter. She grasped the two bags and began slowly to climb the winding path upwards. It was not possible to keep hold of the rope, and she soon let it fall, for Ulysses kept close behind her, his ears pointing forwards, and perhaps it was just as well for him that they moved slowly, with frequent halts, while Joanna struggled to recover from each lap with great heavy breaths. "Oh my dear soul," she uttered once, when it looked as if they would never make it to the top: the higher they climbed, the farther there was to go. "Why did I choose Santorini, of all places? We might at least have met each other on a flat island!"

Near the top, they began to see villagers, widows in black with shawls over their heads, who looked with amazement at the approaching caravan, a shameless woman in gaudy pants leading a donkey whom she had neglected to the point of cruelty. Joanna longed to explain, but by now she had no breath even to speak to Ulysses. She just dropped her eyes, and looked at the stones under her feet, counting steps, and resting after every two hundred, to look down at the serene blue harbor, so far below.

The sunlight reflected sharply off the white houses and

Joanna felt dizzy. "I shall have to have some coffee, Ulysses. And find water for you," she said. The thought of coffee led her on, up the last hairpin curve to the final parapet. There she sat down heavily on a stone step, unable to go further. Ulysses stood two steps below her, so it happened that she could look straight into his face for the first time and saw how beautiful and dark his eyes were, rimmed in long lashes; and again she laid a hand gently on his forehead and caressed his soft nose. When she did this, his drooping ears pricked, and he bent his head a little. But unfortunately she could also now see, even better than before, how dreadful the sores on his belly were. She brushed a fly away from his right eye, and watched it go and settle on the oozing blood. And she gave a sigh that came from deep down, a sigh in which fear before what she had undertaken, and pity and loathing of the suffering she had witnessed, all came together and lay around her heart like a heavy weight.

Her arrival at Santorini was very different from what she had imagined when she left Athens that morning, but it was completely in character.

CHAPTER 2

They had reached the top, but this was only the beginning of a day in which the name Ulysses seemed to have been only too prophetic. No doubt she herself looked queer enough to the peasant women entirely covered in thick black skirts with black kerchiefs covering their heads, a tropical bird flown down into their midst. Perhaps they could understand the bundle of easel and canvases, but they could not understand the donkey. Sometimes her tale got a shy smile, but then always the wrinkled faces closed and the old heads shook: "No, we have no room for a donkey. Besides, it would eat the garden." On Santorini where every drop of water and earth has had to be lifted up in kegs, and each tomato plant and each flower which survives is a sort of miracle, the idea of an all-devouring donkey, a useless pet, was an extravagance they simply could not condone. The answer had been "no" so many times that finally, as the sun was setting and the whole bay below suffused with deep rose, Joanna sat down on the steps of the village bakery and—thoroughly ashamed of herself—cried. She pulled the donkey's head toward her and let the tears fall on it in a total abandonment of hope.

"Oh my dear, dear, what are we going to do now?" She wept, and it seemed as if all the tears she had held back through the war were now falling in abandon on Ulysses' head. His eyes were half-closed. He had eaten half a slice of bread, and drunk a little water she had begged for him. But he must be so tired himself. And she had been so determined to find a haven, a place to sleep, that she had done nothing about his sores. She felt at this moment a heap of female weakness, a useless foolish woman, a *sentimental* woman, she told herself. This last self-hurled insult roused her pride. She wiped her eyes and turned her head upward. The baker was getting ready to close his door. And suddenly she was furious.

"It's a monstrous village," she said. "I have begged shelter all afternoon and you close your doors. Monsters! Heathen!" she shouted at the baker, a big man with a full black beard and a red mouth, now open with astonishment. He was not used to meeting the furies on his doorstep, this sedate bourgeois of the village.

"Look!" She pointed at the donkey. "He's sick. And I'm exhausted."

The man scratched his head in a bewildered way.

"What am I to do?" he asked rather meekly.

"Find us somewhere to sleep, or you won't sleep your-self!" She was standing now and looking straight at his dark eyes which glowed with a faint ruby light and re-minded her of the eyes of a small bull. Then suddenly she laughed.

It was the laugh, perhaps, that did it.

"I know I'm a fool," she admitted, "but even fools have a right to shelter."

The baker was frowning as if the invention of a place to sleep were an effort such as that Zeus himself made when he created Pallas Athene. Then the light slowly broke; the red mouth opened to show astonishingly white teeth.

"Would you mind sleeping in a chapel?" he asked. "Just tonight?"

"A chapel?" Joanna asked, feeling bewildered. Would they allow a donkey in a church, even though he did, like all his fellows, bear the mark of the cross on his back, an uneven cross, as if stroked in with a rough brush?

"It's a little one; my family built it to give thanks when my mother's uncle was rescued in a storm. But the roof doesn't leak" (as if it would rain!) "and the walls are thick." He began to warm to his own plan. "I can lend you some sheepskins."

"Oh yes, yes!" Joanna cried. "A little chapel is just what we need."

"Wait a minute." The baker disappeared into his shop and came back with a loaf of bread and the sheepskins over his arm. "It's yesterday's, but it's yours if you want it."

While he turned back to lock the door, Joanna wanted very much to give the donkey a large hunk of bread, but she was afraid of shocking the baker out of his kindness. "Just wait, Ulysses, it is going to be all right," she whispered into one of his ears.

The baker did not offer to help her, so she lifted the two bags and the easel once more, and followed meekly behind his comforting bulk. It seemed an interminable journey; in the course of it she dropped the donkey's rope, but he followed after, his head nodding, as if he were half asleep. Finally in a field above the village, they came to a small square white building with a round dome and a cross on it, like hundreds of others she had seen without ever imagining that she would one day sleep in one with a donkey.

The door creaked open into a dazzling darkness. But there was still a little light in the sky. She let the bags fall with immense relief—there they could lie for the night anyway.

The baker was showing off his chapel as if it were a palace. He had suddenly become the host and she an honored guest. He showed her where she might sleep on a rise in the earthen floor where presumably the altar had once been. He was arranging the sheepskins now upon this, and as he stood to leave, she caught a suddenly human twinkle in his bull's blank gaze.

"My great uncle, God rest his soul, would have enjoyed the thought of a pretty woman sleeping in his chapel. Come in!" he roared at the donkey who was standing, drooping, in the doorway as if waiting for an invitation. "Great Uncle would not have approved of you, but he'll never know, so come in."

But Ulysses waited for Joanna to give a slight tug to his collar before he stepped daintily inside.

"There," said the baker.

He seemed as delighted as if he had led them into a palace. "Sweet dreams!"

Joanna watched him go down the field and drop out of sight among the flat roofs of the village below.

"Well, here we are, Ulysses," she said, breaking off a great hunk of bread. "This is for you."

She felt the soft lips nibbling at her hand, and was grateful when he swallowed a few bites. But Ulysses was not as hungry as she was. Poor beast, tomorrow we'll get some salve and cure you, she thought. Now we must sleep, we must sleep. She had never been so tired in her whole life, nor so hungry. She pulled off pieces of bread and ate while she opened up a bag and finally found the flashlight. Perhaps this was a mistake as when she turned it on the walls, a dozen huge cockroaches scuttled away. Joanna would have preferred really to find herself in a lion's den than in a cockroach-infested chapel. Sleep fled. She lay down on the sheepskins with the flashlight in her hand and played it around every five minutes—and in the dark intervals imagined a cockroach walking across her hand or neck.

Meanwhile Ulysses stood perfectly still, his eyes closed, his head drooping, and perhaps he slept.

Nevertheless, white night though it was, she had lost the sense of utter desolation and abandonment that had taken hold of her on the baker's front steps.

"After all, we have shelter, Ulysses, and a loaf of bread. That is, perhaps, more than a mad woman and a sick donkey could expect." She felt her way to the door, opened it and stole out. It must have been about midnight. The stars looked huge, as huge as daisies, and so bright that she could see each stone in the field, and the roofs of the village looked like a magic city, below.

In spite of the drama of the day, into which she had thrown herself with such intensity that there had hardly been space in which to analyse what was happening to her, Joanna felt strangely at peace. However preposterous the adventure, it was related in some way to the inner person . . . and this was true in spite of the fact that she had at first winced before taking on a gratuitous responsibility, when, after all, she had set out early that morning, so long ago, in search of freedom, determined to be committed only to her self, the Joanna who had wanted to cry her identity aloud to the sea gulls. Well, perhaps, Ulysses was a kind of answer to that un-uttered cry. She had taken to herself already a part of the natural world; she had indulged in a private madness, and, for once, the gods seemed to be smiling at bravado.

While down below the secret village slept, here she was as wide awake as an owl, filled with excitement, and at the same time at peace. Already her fingers were itching for charcoal and canvas. She stood there, wrapped in a sheepskin, for the air was cold, and knew her joy. It breathed through her in a long sigh, the sigh of a person who lets fall heavy clothing onto the ground. Within, she heard the donkey relieving himself.

"Dear soul, you are safe," she murmured, and perhaps it was spoken to herself as well as to the donkey, for perhaps she too had been in need of rescue.

CHAPTER 3

Towards daybreak, Joanna must have slept, for she was woken by a terrific noise, ear-splitting, a noise she did not at first recognize—she leapt up, wide awake, and terrified, only to realize suddenly that the noise, which was loud and monstrous enough to come from an elephant in distress, was merely Ulysses greeting the dawn!

"Either you are feeling much better, or much worse," she said, putting her arms round his neck and leaning her forehead against his forehead. At this instant his bray was answered by a chorus of other donkeys below in the town. Here, high up, he had been the first to welcome the sun through a crack in the door. His breath made white puffs in the semi-dark.

Joanna opened the door and shivered with pleasure. It

was a perfect morning world, the sea soft and silken blue and the sky still flushed with rose. The air itself was like some strange nourishment, a tonic, and she drew in deep breaths and stretched her arms over her head. Yesterday had been a nightmare, but today would be quite different, she decided. When she had combed her hair, and found a clean shirt in her luggage, she tied Ulysses to the door, and walked slowly down to the village alone. When she got to the end of the field where the path made a sharp dip, she turned back to wave. Ulysses looked awfully small and frail standing there, but he did not strain on the rope, as if he knew she would come back soon.

First she went to a taverna and drank three cups of bitter black coffee. She had to admit to herself that life became much easier without the donkey. People who had frowned the day before gave her the island greeting now, and the owner of the taverna, a young man with a limp, even offered to help her find a place to stay. "No wonder painters come to Santorini, it is so beautiful," he said, looking down into the bay far below where one yacht lay at anchor. When she paid him, she found that she did after all have several thousand drachma left. She had the address of an old woman who sometimes rented a room in her house, and the young man accompanied her part of the way to the druggist's so she would not get lost in the labyrinthine white streets. But she did not tell him why she needed the druggist's help. She who had never been wily until the war, now knew how to be wily, and that was a lucky thing for the donkey.

The druggist was sleepy and disgruntled. "What do you want?" he asked in a grumbly voice, "so early in the morning?"

"I want salve for an open wound."

His heavy black eyebrows knitted together. "Gun-shot?"

"No, I scraped my knee. It has not healed."

He peered down at her tight trousers, and the beetling brows which had frowned now made arcs of astonishment.

"Oh?" he said, and smiled a secretive smile. "It should be bandaged, of course." He sniffed his contempt of elegant Athenian women whom vanity kept from bandaging a sore knee.

"Do you have bandages?" she asked meekly.

"Yes," he nodded and began to open dusty wooden drawers behind him, rummaging about, and finally drawing forth a roll of bandage with a large red cross on the paper. He winked. "War matériel."

She looked at the splendid big roll longingly, but when the druggist, whose interest was warming up, brought out a tiny tube of salve about an inch and a half long, she was dismayed. It would never cover Ulysses' belly, only a fraction of it, and in her mind's eye she saw the horrible black icing of flies. "Oh dear."

"What's wrong? This is the best there is. I guarantee it." He saw that she was worried. "It is expensive, of course. Everything is expensive these days," and he shrugged his shoulders.

"Yes, of course . . . yes. I'll take four tubes," she said in a loud determined voice.

"Four tubes? Are you crazy?" The man laughed aloud.

"I am always getting scratched, hauling my painting things about on the rocks. I would like to have a reserve."

"Well take five, take six!" The very thought of so many tubes of precious salve seemed to make him angry. "What do I care?"

"Yes, perhaps six would be better," she said dreamily. Every time she considered Ulysses' belly it seemed to grow bigger and even six tubes seemed hardly enough.

All the time, while the druggist wrapped up the six tubes and the bandage in an old newspaper and tied it with an end of string he found in one of the drawers, he was muttering curses and prayers to himself. "Mad, utterly mad, holy Jesus and Mary, forgive us our sins. Protect us from the evil eye."

She couldn't wait to get away, and when she did, ran down the street like a thief with her precious bundle, not daring to look back, though she was certain he must be standing in the door watching her as if she were a wild animal.

When she had turned a corner, she leaned against the wall of a house, panting. Then the absurdity of her situation dawned and she laughed aloud. An old woman, feeling her way down the street with a stick, paused in amazement.

For the rest of the way to the house the tavern-keeper had suggested, she kept her head down and tried to look like a respectable citizen. And she must have succeeded because in a few minutes she had rented a small dark room in the old woman's house for a month. The room was small, but the bed looked clean and there was not a cockroach in sight. There was also a small garden in front where a few roses and calendulas bloomed, and where Joanna imagined Ulysses in an Italian straw hat with a necklace of blue beads round his neck, peacefully munching—not the flowers, of course, but hay. She must see to that.

The old woman counted the drachmas in her hand with visible satisfaction. "God has sent you," she said, smiling a toothless smile. Her eyes were such a milky brown that Joanna thought she must be almost blind.

"Well, I am glad, too," said Joanna, "for I slept in an abandoned chapel last night and was devoured by cockroaches."

"In a chapel? The saints preserve us! And weren't you afraid?"

"I didn't have time to be afraid, I guess."

The old woman shook her head. These Athenians, they were afraid of nothing. She imagined there were no ghosts in Athens, it was too noisy and crowded perhaps. And she watched the strange girl in her gaudy trousers run down the street to get her baggage. It's early in the season and God is good, the old woman thought to herself. She is rich, a painter, and she paid the whole month in advance. I can't lose.

It was nearly eleven by the time Joanna appeared over the steep declivity from the field . . . would Ulysses still be there? The sun felt hot now and she feared the heat would be bad for his sores. But she was too occupied with pushing and trundling a small bale of hay up the path to do more than make sure he was still there. Her idea was to keep the hay here in the chapel and bring Ulysses up every morning. Then he would be out of the way (those flowers!).

"There," she said with one last heave. "It's for you, Ulysses."

Already his neck was stretched out pulling at the rope; he was hungry and that was a good sign. Only now she faced the fear she had had that he might die in the night. She looked down and saw the sores still bleeding, still covered in a black foam of flies. "We must get to work, my friend."

While Ulysses pulled at the hay and munched methodically, Joanna opened up the bandage and sat down as close to his belly as she could get. It had, she noticed, an awful smell of sickness and decay. Would he kick her if she tried to touch him there? Still, it was essential to get the flies off; she waved her hands and they rose briefly, then settled again to their bloody feast. Nausea rose in her throat.

There was nothing to do but go at it and hope for the best. She opened one tube of salve and squeezed frantically; the minute her hand touched the sore, Ulysses shivered. His whole skin reacted as at the prick of a pin.

"I can't help it," she admonished him. "It is going to hurt."

Then she gritted her teeth and smeared a full tube all over the worst place. Ulysses, after that first tremor of fear, stayed quite still. He stopped munching. His ears drooped forwards, but he seemed to know what she was doing, and put on his ancient cloak of patient suffering. Once he turned his head toward her and she saw the marvelous deep brown eye looking at her, as if he were saying "it hurts, but I am grateful." And pretty soon she had forgotten her fear of being kicked and went about the sorry business as deftly and quickly as she could. When his whole under-belly was covered with salve, she unrolled the bandage and wound it round him. Alas, it only went halfway and she realized that she must find burlap bags, string, something that would keep the wounds covered. Still, she had learned that a donkey can understand and bear a great deal. She would not be afraid again.

"You are going to get well," she said, when she got up and could stroke his ears. "You are going to be the healthiest beast on Santorini."

The salve smelled strongly of antiseptic. She could almost feel its healing powers. But she had used up all six tubes in one dressing. However explain to the druggist tomorrow that she would need six more, and the next day six more? How long would it take, she wondered in a panic? Ten days? Twenty days?

CHAPTER 4

She had been so absorbed for the last twenty-four hours that she had nearly forgotten her promise to her father to write at once, and she had altogether forgotten that she had not come to Santorini to become a donkey-nurse. If she did not now devise a plan for the days ahead, and keep herself to it, she could see how lightly and nonchalantly the whole precious month might just slip away.

"I have to work, Ulysses," she told him, pulling one of his ears. The other ear pricked forward as if he was listening hard. "Yes, I have to work," she said, letting the other soft ear slide through her fingers. The top of the donkey's head was already warm and she could feel the brilliant sunlight hot on her own neck. At the base of the ears, Ulysses' head felt damp—fever? But of course she must

[37

buy him a straw hat! "Come along," she said, suddenly impatient to solve what seemed like a million small problems, to get away from thoughts of a hat, and—oh yes—a necklace of blue beads such as all well-dressed donkeys wear, not only for decorative purposes but to keep away evil spirits. Perhaps if she bought him a blanket, she could manage to rest the easel on his back, and if he could carry this light burden it would make the daily search for a place to paint a great deal easier.

"Come along," she said, giving the rope a tug. "We have an immeasurable amount to do and first of all I must write a postcard to Papa!"

Luckily she was now so determined to dispatch all errands that she quite forgot how the village might look at her apparition among them with a sick donkey at her heels. She hardly noticed the stares that accompanied her passage first to the post office, then to thank the baker for his kindness, and to buy a fresh loaf of bread, some cheese and a few tomatoes, for she felt extraordinarily light and hungry. They would end up at her lodgings, she decided, and there she would eat and perhaps have a siesta. Then in the evening light she might summon the strength to go back once more, collect all the luggage, and sit down and think with her sketch book, for "thinking" to Joanna meant drawing something. Perhaps that broken-down stone wall on the way down. Perhaps . . . she lit a cigarette and leaned for a moment in the cool shadow of a house. Although she was standing quite still, and looked quite relaxed, she was actually beginning to feel a wild impa-

tience to get to work. It was as if her whole equilibrium
were shifting and some inner tension being set up which
she could not control in any way except by sitting down
and concentrating all her powers. In this state she found
herself analysing everything she looked at in terms of
mass, texture, light, and shade. She now focused her gaze
on the wall of the house opposite, at the diagonal shadow
that cut across the rough wall.

At that moment Ulysses suddenly sneezed.

"My dear soul, are you cold?" It was true she had forgotten all about his hat, his blanket, his blue beads! And
off they went in search of a shop which specialized in
donkey-wear. In a village like Santorini where there are
as many donkeys as people, Joanna did not have far to go.
She pushed her way into a dark room rather like Aladdin's
cave—such a flash of buckles and straps and belts and
bunches of blue beads hanging from the ceiling, and such
an array of hats, hanging like huge flowers all around her!

"Hey," the shopkeeper called out, "don't let him in!"
For Ulysses had pushed his soft nose in behind her.

"He's perfectly gentle."

"Gentle, maybe—but he'll eat the hats!"

Joanna laughed. "He doesn't want to eat a hat, he wants
to wear one," she said, busily examining a splendid one
with a red rose at one side, holes for ears of course, one
that seemed to give ample shade. "May I try it on?" she
asked, as the shopkeeper seemed someone easily offended.

It slipped on as if it had been made especially for
Ulysses, and Joanna walked a few steps away to look at

[39

it critically; then she couldn't help laughing, for it was absurdly becoming, only it made the rest of poor Ulysses look naked suddenly, incongruous in the rough bandage tied with string. His ears drooped and he shook his head, and Joanna ran to hug him and to tell him that she was not actually laughing *at* him, he must understand.

"Yes," she said, "I'll take that one, but we must have something to put on his back. A blanket or perhaps something with bags so he could help me carry my easel and painting things?"

The shopkeeper, aware that he had been handed a good thing, bustled about and produced magnificent moroccan saddle bags of tooled leather with red and gold tassels.

"How much?" Joanna asked. "No, they are too expensive for us," she said, giggling suddenly, "prices would go up wherever we were seen." She had the image of a sort of Rolls Royce donkey, so grand that she would have to change her whole style of living. "Don't even tell me. I am a painter and painters are not rich."

"Even in Athens where everyone is rich?" the shop-keeper teased her. "I will make you a bargain."

"No," Joanna put her hands to her ears. "Let me see the saddle bags of Santorini, those all the donkeys wear—"

"We are not weavers," he grunted. "Go to Mykonos for that." And he threw down some coarse handwoven saddle bags, with a bold black and white design.

"That's it. That's perfect," Joanna cried, imagining each bag bulging with paints, loaves of bread, even hay. Everything had become real again, believable. She would be able to cure Ulysses, and paint. But just to be sure that she would not now be punished for her pride, she hastily chose a particularly splendid collar of blue beads with a pendant hanging from it made of leather decorated with tiny white and yellow beads.

Of course these first days were bound to be expensive, she consoled herself, as she handed out two more big bills. "Once we have settled down, we can live on nothing," she assured Ulysses. She laid the saddle bags over his back, and knelt to arrange the necklace around his neck.

"There," she said, "now you are beautiful as well as wise."

It was the shopkeeper's turn to laugh.

Joanna was hurt. She turned on him. "I know," she said. "He looks miserable because of his sores. But that is not his fault." She stood and faced the shopkeeper and said quite crossly, "If you had something, some burlap or old cloths I could tie around his belly, it would be a help."

He turned back into the shop, shaking his head, and it was hard to tell whether he had gone for good, or whether . . . Joanna waited a moment—yes, he was coming back.

"Here," he said, tossing two quite clean-looking burlap bags at her. Then, appalled by such an act of generosity, which had been apparently wrenched out of him, in spite of himself, he spat, and turned back without a further word, as if he didn't want her thanks.

"Now, home, Ulysses!" she said, giving the rope a tug. She heard the cheerful clatter of the little hooves behind her; Ulysses was actually trotting!

The old woman was sitting in front of her house on a chair, knitting a sock, and watching the street for her new tenant. When she saw what looked like a gypsy caravan arriving, she could not believe her eyes. A donkey—and what a donkey! Half dead, and dressed up as if for a funeral—his own, no doubt. And where was the luggage?

"Here I am," Joanna said. "We are going to have something to eat, and a siesta, and then we will go and get the luggage."

The old woman heard "we" but did not take it in.

"But—but—" she muttered, looking down, and wiping her hands absent-mindedly on her apron. "But . . ."

"His name is Ulysses," Joanna said. "I am trying to heal his sores, and then we shall see. I know, I didn't tell you I had a donkey," she added. "But he will be no trouble."

The old woman cast an apprehensive eye at her flowers.

"I'll pay for any damage he does."

The old woman stood there, silently, and Joanna waited.

"We'll be off painting all day," she said pleadingly. Oh please, she prayed silently, don't stop me now. Don't spoil the day. I do so want to get started.

"Look," Joanna said, in a determined voice which surprised her by its firmness. "I'll just fasten his rope to the shutter here, and he'll do no harm, surely."

She had received neither a yes nor a no, when she went into the house and closed the door behind her on her dark room. She found it an immense relief to be alone, to be unseen. Once there, she lay down on the bed, her hands under her head, and stared at the ceiling, and for the first time the excitement and demands of her adventure, which had kept her going until this moment, fell away and she faced the fact that Ulysses was going to ask her endurance as well as her love. She felt rather overwhelmed, until she remembered that the real trouble was that she was hungry. It was wonderful what a difference bread, cheese, and tomatoes could make in a person's state of mind. When she had eaten, she lay down and buried her head in the pillow and was fast asleep before she knew it.

It was past four o'clock when she woke with a start, not remembering where she was, nor what she was doing. She put her hands in the precious jug of water on the stand in a corner of the room and then cooled off her face with her wet hands. It had been a magic sleep: she knew exactly what she wanted to do. When one has been starved for a long time, one wants first very simple food, bread and milk. It seemed to Joanna that what she must do was get back to the corner of broken stone wall from which a steep cliff dropped straight down to the lapis-still sea—must sit and look at it and sense its shape, its substance, the worn rounded shapes of the stones, the texture of it, and the small bouquet of grasses that had managed to grow in an interstice. The need to set down just what this felt like in her fingers was imperative.

The light, when she pushed open the door, was dazzling, and for a second she could see nothing. Then what she saw was too amazing to take in at first glance. Not a single one of the roses and calendulas in their low stone boxes had been left; Ulysses was standing, innocently, beside the denuded boxes quietly munching the remains of his hat. The rose disappeared as Joanna gave a cry of despair, but she could not help laughing just the same.

"Oh how could you do it? You wretched donkey!"

Ulysses pricked his ears toward her and turned his head and gave her a long, dark, tender look. It was clear that he had spent a very enjoyable afternoon.

CHAPTER 5

If Ulysses showed exemplary patience, so did Joanna. And as one colossally blue hot day rose and flowered and faded, they slowly achieved a way of living together, and the village too accepted the woman and her donkey; the chemist no longer experienced shock when Joanna bought twelve tubes of salve every two days; the old woman decided that money might be as good as flowers; and the baker agreed to allow the donkey to be tethered to the chapel at night provided that he ate only hay bought by Joanna and did not crop the few bits of dried grass in the field.

Ulysses did not devour his second Italian hat which bore no such temptation as a rich red rose on it this time, but only a severe dark blue rosette instead. And slowly the sores healed, and here and there a patch of soft curly hair grew in on his belly. The days settled into a rhythm, as Joanna began to walk (rather than run) about her business, began to take deep breaths, began to relax. By half past eight—after the regular routine of three cups of black coffee and a walk to the chapel, where she rubbed salve into Ulysses' wounds and re-bandaged him, and took him to drink at the village well—they were off. The village people had grown accustomed to seeing the odd procession, the tall woman in her garish trousers, followed by the tiny donkey in a straw hat, bearing an easel and a paintbox on his back, a loaf of bread emerging from one saddle bag and sometimes a bottle of wine from the other. Once in a while a little boy scrambled up the rocks beside her, and stood watching while she set up her easel.

"Why do you paint stones?" one of these ragged ones asked, his eyes bright and curious. "Why not the village?"

"Because I am clumsy," Joanna answered. "I have to begin with first things. I can see the stones; I cannot yet see the village."

One bare foot scraped against the other while he considered this, and then considered Ulysses, who was delicately sniffing his way among the dry bushes, hoping to uncover some unexpected delicacy.

"How long will you stay here?"

The question flew down so swiftly, it took Joanna by surprise. It seemed to stay there like an ominous bird settling on her easel.

"It's a holiday. Holidays are not very long."

48]

There was a silence. Already the sun began to burn. The scent of thyme breathed up from the ground.

"I have to work now," Joanna said.

"Why do you have to, if it's a holiday?"

"It's like fishing. Do you like to fish?"

"I go with my father to fish."

"And it's a holiday . . . ?"

"But we sell the fish," he said proudly. "People eat them."

Joanna smiled. "Only Ulysses eats my paintings now and then, I'm afraid." Ulysses had developed an appetite for sketchbook paper, although he preferred ice cream.

"Does Ulysses live with you in Athens?"

"You must run along now," Joanna said quite sharply. For the child had hit on something she refused to think about this week . . . what to do with Ulysses when the time came?

"Yes," the boy agreed. "I'll go now. Only tell me: if this is like fishing, what are you fishing for?"

For a second Joanna laid down the black crayon in her hand, and stood looking out over the stubby pasture, so barren and spacious, high up over the sea. "It's a good question," she said seriously. "Let me think it over."

"Very well," he said, "you can tell me tomorrow," and he was off down the field. After a few moments, Joanna could hear him whistling, a shrill whistling song. For a second she felt lonely. The child had filled the landscape with his presence as if he had been a small god. Now she felt the emptiness, the solitude all around her. And far off in the distance the whistling sounded strangely melancholy, in this early morning world so austere—and so demanding.

"What am I fishing for?" she murmured, picking up the black pencil. Within an hour such questions had become irrelevant. She had torn up three attempts and was sitting cross-legged on the ground smoking a cigarette. Ulysses, hearing the sound of crumpled paper, trotted up, and stood munching beside her. "You are a vacuum cleaner," said Joanna, and he rubbed her back with his head. He was apt to come and do this two or three times in a morning, as if to say, "Good to find you still here."

"Yes, I'm here," she answered then, rubbing his nose. "But I'm stuck, Ulysses, thoroughly and absolutely stuck."

She had been trying altogether too hard this morning. For it was a fact that one caught no fish by trying too hard. She turned over on her stomach and pulled the big straw hat down over her eyes. Ulysses stood over her, quite still. Every now and then she could feel his warm breath on her back. And in her doze Joanna was thinking in the only way she knew, as a painter thinks.

Just before noon, when the light had become so white and dazzling that it seemed quite hopeless to see anything, let alone draw it (draw the center of a flame?), she found herself setting down almost as if it were a memory, and not what in fact she had been looking at all morning, a piece of broken wall with a single delicate tuft of flowers growing through a crevice. And this she did not tear up. "Why am I fishing?" she asked herself, as she screwed up her eyes one last time, and then laid down the pencil.

"Because if I can see these stones and this tuft of grass with absolute clarity, for itself alone, I somehow feel clear in myself."

When she and Ulysses had shared the loaf of bread and she had eaten a tomato and a hunk of goat cheese and washed it all down with two glasses of wine, Joanna wrote a letter to her father. Until now it had been hard not to mention Ulysses. She was here to paint—not to become an Animal Rescue League. She was well aware that a letter about Ulysses, read in an apartment in Athens, would somehow lose its reality. Better wait and see before mentioning anything so disturbing to her father, alone and feeling his loneliness acutely.

So she wrote. "You know the islands. I do not need to tell you the sort of field I sit in, high up over the village, a field of broken stone walls and stubble, where one finds pure elation, because of the height, because of the amazing clear air (now at noon, it burns like flame) and the shimmering blue of the sea far below. The sea is the only extravagance in all this austerity. I have not yet dared to contemplate it as a painter. I am painting nothing but stones, broken stone walls, tufts of grass, and flowers. What I want is absolute reality and poetry at the same time. The poetry must never be vague or romantic, but to come from exactitude, severity, more than an *atmosphere*, if you understand what I am trying to say. You ask whether I am lonely. Not at all. I miss you, of course, and the books and carpets and paintings and all the richness of our life together in Athens. But, just for the moment, all this seems

[51

irrelevant. I am stripped down to an essential life. You said I looked like a gypsy; it is more true now; I am toasted brown. I live between the extraordinary light up here in the fields where I paint, and my closed sealed room in a peasant's house in the village. There I have a bed, a chair, a washstand; it is always cool and always dark. I sleep all afternoon, and then go out again after four when the shadows begin to give some form to what is now only glare. You know better than I that I shall never be a painter. I shall never, alas, warm your pride with a show in Athens, nor dazzle a single critic into being my champion. And you might well ask, as a little boy this morning asked, who had followed me up from the village, filled with curiosity, 'What are you doing all this *for*? What are you fishing for?' Yet this morning I achieved something for myself. I knew happiness. Dear father, you have wished other things for me. You have hoped I would marry. I too have sometimes hoped for marriage. But what I want to say, as I sit here, with a straw hat pulled down over my eyes against the white light that dazzles, is that I take a Greek pride in devoting myself to the impossible, and that (perhaps) there lies joy . . . if I had become a professional painter with all that implies of competition and status, I might never have found the joy that was with me this morning when I *saw* the essence of a few stones and was able to communicate it, at least to myself."

Joanna felt Ulysses' head, rubbing gently against her back. This time, she knew it meant "it is time for our siesta." And, up to a point obedient, she got up and began to stow the paraphernalia on his back. "I wonder, Ulysses, would I have had the courage to climb so high without your help?"

They went slowly, in the heat of noon, each under his protecting hat, down to the village where the preoccupations of that morning would have seemed ludicrous indeed.

CHAPTER 6

Down in the village, Joanna
was observed, as are all
creatures without a mate, with a mixture of scorn and
envy. In the cafés, over the ritual glass of ouzo as the sun
set, the men occasionally talked about her as a mysteri-
ous being; full-breasted, narrow-legged, aloof, she walked
among them with a distant air which made the young
men uneasy and the old men remember ribald jokes they
had not told for years. And they resented Ulysses, rescued,
pampered, and apparently dearer to this strange creature
than any of them would ever be. A woman alone and who
seems happy to be alone arouses mixed emotions; she
threatens something people do not talk about, and if she is
not very lucky indeed she will be punished in one way or
another for being a threat.

[55

Fortunately perhaps, Joanna was not aware of the emotions she aroused. "Come, angel," she would say to Ulysses as they walked down the village street, with no idea what reverberations that "angel" addressed to a small no-account donkey left in her wake. But she would not have denied that Ulysses was taking a rather large space in her consciousness. Her father, in his increasing nervousness and captiousness since the tragedies of the war, had not wanted a pet. Perhaps it was a necessary part of his closing off the sensitive and innocent part of himself which had died with her mother; to open that secret being would be too painful. What is it about animals? Joanna wondered as she stroked the soft nose of Ulysses and looked into his deep brown eye, so tender and yet so remote. Is it that animals rest and nourish some deep natural being in us; they make us young and merry again; they restore us to childhood's world, pure and self-absorbed . . . and they do this partly because the means of communication are so very simple, a meal, a caress . . . even Ulysses' sores had been a simple matter compared to the deep wounds of human beings, which even a ton of the most expensive salve cannot cure. At any rate, Joanna was quite convinced that the companionship of Ulysses, despite all the time he consumed, was a good thing for the painter. Those hands which found pleasure in touching his furry face, in slipping his long ears through them, seemed extra-sensitized when they held a brush, as if the sensual world, locked away for years, was being woken. Joy, the most elusive of all feelings, the rarest, was in the air.

"But what, oh what shall I do with you when I have to go, my little vacuum cleaner?"

And just because this was such an insoluble question, Joanna refused to allow it to break into her happiness for the moment. In two weeks . . . maybe. After all, anything may happen in two weeks. But for the time being she was going to savor every hour of this miraculous holiday.

She had acquired a friend in the last few days . . . the little boy was apt to appear sometime during the morning, although she often went off on expeditions that took her right to the other side of the island. It had become a game for him, she suspected, to track her down, and when he appeared suddenly on a high rock above her or raced along the cliff edge, he shouted and waved as if she were some long-lost treasure. Sometimes she heard his lonely haunting whistle far off, carried by the wind, although he was nowhere in sight. And when he leaped down the rocks to her side, his whole face one huge smile, she had got into the habit of sharing her lunch with him. For one thing, she didn't mind talking while she was eating, but she did not want to be distracted during her work time. So they sat on a warm ledge, side by side, with Ulysses sometimes bending down long ears between them to catch a nibble of the tomatoes which he loved.

The little boy asked the question which no doubt the older men in the village bandied about among themselves. Did he relate her answers when he swaggered down the village street, big with secrets? Well, if he did, Joanna did not mind. She only told him the truth.

When he asked, "Why are you alone?" scanning her face with such intensity (she felt sometimes as if his eyes were nibbling at her as Ulysses' soft lips sometimes actually did)—when he asked this fundamental question, she took a long swallow of *retsina*, and looked out at the long sweep of blue bay below them.

"I wonder," she answered half to herself. "Why am I alone?"

"Don't you *know*?" The voice was shrill with surprise and disappointment.

Joanna laughed then and turned the question on him, "Why are you alone, do you suppose?"

He looked at her askance then with the wild blank look of a goat.

"I'm not alone. I live with my father and my mother and two sisters."

"But you are alone here, now, and all day sometimes, aren't you?"

"I want to see things for myself. I want to know . . ." he frowned. "I want to be myself."

"Well then, so do I. I too live with my father, but sometimes I have to get away to be myself."

He watched gravely while she broke off another piece of cheese and handed it to him with a piece of bread. For a moment they each chewed in silence. Then Ulysses gave a loud sigh—something between a sigh and a rude cheer, blowing the breath out loudly through his nose. It meant, you have forgotten me.

"Here, here's a tomato for you," said Joanna, and then they all three munched for a while.

"But . . ." the little boy began again when he had swallowed and burped. "You are a woman. Women marry."

"It's as simple as that, little donkey?"

"I'm not a donkey," the little boy answered, flushing. "In the village, they talk about why you are not married."

"Oh, and what do they say in the village?"

"Some say you are queer, a witch, they say. They say you are proud, an Athenian woman with her nose in the air."

"They can say what they please," Joanna said. She felt suddenly exposed. The solitude she had imagined she was experiencing had been an illusion then. In fact she was bound to every pair of curious eyes that watched her go down the street from behind closed shutters. I am their prey, she thought with violent distaste. And I do not belong here.

"But you could tell me," the little boy pleaded. "I too ask why you are not married."

He stood his ground, looking her straight in the eyes.

For just a second a wave of blackness fell between Joanna's eyes and the world around her, and she felt dizzy. The past that she had willed to leave behind her now flooded back, and the pain was so acute, that she instinctively pressed her hand to her heart.

"I came to Santorini to forget for a while," she said, when she opened her eyes. "Look at the sea, how peaceful it is."

"Yes, it is peaceful," said the little boy.

He took a stone and threw it as far as he could, a gesture in which there was some anger.

And Joanna felt that she was being tugged back, in spite of herself, drawn back into the complex human world. For a little while she had been allowed to escape with Ulysses into the partial world of animals. Now she was being suddenly asked by a little dirty boy to grow up all in a moment from the animal world, from the world of poetry, where the stones had been speaking to her but no human being had addressed her as a human being . . . she was being asked now to answer for her *self*. And how could she answer for her self, without telling the whole long story, the buried story? But straight questions require straight answers. Why indeed had she not married?

"Sit down, Nicholas," she said gently. It was the first time she had called him by his name. Until now he had been in her mind just "the boy," as he might have been "the donkey" or "the stone." And this was true although he had told her his name some days ago.

He sat cross-legged in front of her, his dark eyes once more concentrated on her face, with that total attention she had come to dread. It asked too much, she felt, more, perhaps than she had to give.

"You do not remember the war, little Nicholas," she began.

"No," he frowned, and then smiled proudly, "but I remember the earthquake!"

"You do, do you?"

"Yes, I remember how our dog howled all the day before

and the cats in the village miaowed, and the stillness. I remember . . . half the village fell into the sea!" he said with pride as if this fantastic phenomenon and terror had been a sort of glory. "The destroyers could not get in for days . . . there was no water."

"War is like that," Joanna told him, and he nodded. "It is an earthquake."

They sat side by side looking down on the stretched silk bay far below, and it was easier to talk because Nicholas no longer stared at her face but he too was looking out over the sea as if he sensed that one does not look grief in the eye.

"You see, my mother . . . Oh it is a long story . . ." at this moment the story lay on her shoulders like a burden heavier than she could carry. After all, when it was all over, they had never talked of it, she and her father. They had buried it in silence, because that seemed the only way to go on. They must not look back, or looking back would become an illness. Instead of thinking, she, Joanna, had stood in lines for coal, for meat, for potatoes, for infinitesimal amounts of fat which was often rancid by the time it reached Athens via the Red Cross or some other charitable organization. She learned how to stand for long hours, and not think, stand like an animal, head bent, just waiting. And she learned to come home and make her father eat, by becoming a nurse with a small child who was pining away. She had scrubbed the floors and done the laundry, had invented impossible tasks, just to be sure she would fall into bed so tired that she could sleep.

And all this, she saw now, so high up and free, had been an evasion, the tricks of a coward. She had allowed herself to become allied with her father on the side of death. For some reason the image which rose up between her and the flat blue sea was the image of her mother coming up the path, waving a great bunch of wild red anemones and crying out to the family, "I know, I'm late, and you must be famished. But look what I have . . . anemones—the blood of Adonis . . . aren't they a splendor? Look at their dark hearts!" Joanna knew now that she could not answer for her *self* without allowing the past to come back to life, and she was afraid. This precious month of escape, of respite, was it to become, after all, a month of coming back, of return to life with all the pangs of rebirth in it?

She was woken out of her silence by Ulysses who had come to rub his head on her back.

"Nicholas," she said, starting awake. "People who come out of a war like this are changed. They are cut off from the real past as if there were a wall standing there."

"But they are glad to be alive?"

"Yes," she said, tears suddenly starting in her eyes, "they are glad to be alive."

"So . . ." he glanced at her shyly and then away.

"So?"

"So, whatever happened, it is all right now."

"Is it all right that half the village fell into the sea? Will it ever be all right?" She turned on him, with sudden anger.

"We have rebuilt it," he said proudly.

"Bravo, Nicholas, you are a Greek. A Greek like my mother. That is how she would have spoken."

"She died?"

"My mother helped prisoners escape . . . it was danger-ous. She knew that, but one doesn't choose. Things hap-pen. The first one was an English airman with a broken knee. He dragged himself to the back door of the dress shop where she worked. Could she turn him away? And so it began, and so it went on—finally she was caught. By then she had become a leader, as the Germans well knew. So they did not make it easy for her." Joanna got up and began to walk up and down. Ulysses stood there with his ears drooping. And Nicholas was afraid.

"What did they do?"

"They put burning cigarettes in my brother's ears, to make her talk. And my brother screamed 'Don't tell, mother, don't tell!' "

Joanna saw the tears shining in the boy's eyes. His voice came out rather shrill and defiant. "And she didn't tell?"

"No, she did not tell. And finally, when she was no use to them or to anyone else, they shot her."

"I cry because I am proud," said Nicholas, wiping his face with his sleeve. "I am so proud of your mother. I am so proud of your brother."

Joanna went on in a dead voice. "My brother is stone deaf. My father, who was a sensitive man, a man in some ways like a child, has never recovered. For one year I sat by his bed in a dark room while he tried to die himself. You see, little Nicholas, a village can be rebuilt but some-

[63

times people cannot. As long as my father lives, I must stay with him." And she was ashamed now to have laid her burden upon a child, ashamed to see how tense his face was against the tears. So she smiled. "And now you know why I am alone."

"I will tell the old men to shut up," said Nicholas.

Ulysses, who had wandered off, now suddenly stretched out his neck and gave an ear-splitting bray. Coming as it did after the contemplation of so much that was nearly unbearable, it had the effect of making Nicholas laugh and laugh, and his laugh was so infectious that Joanna too heaved with laughter. When Nicholas had caught his breath, he pointed to a donkey far below, tied to a boulder while his master tried to pry out a precious piece of drift-wood from between two rocks.

"He's braying because he saw the donkey!"

And now they saw the other donkey lift his head and send forth an answer, which echoed among the rocks under the silent sky like the voice of some demon in agony. It was very funny—such unholy sounds emerging from such a meek creature, and especially as they were sounds of love.

"Time for a siesta," Joanna said. "Good heavens, yes, it's nearly two o'clock! I am dreadfully sleepy. . . ."

Nicholas looked up at her for a second as if he had something he wanted to say, but decided not to. Instead he ran down the hill, jumping over stones, as if he were rejoicing in his freedom, as if he needed to run like a goat, showing off a little, but when he was out of sight, Joanna heard the melancholy flute whistling its song.

What had happened? she wondered as she walked slowly back toward the village, her straw hat pulled low over her eyes against the glare, and Ulysses rather reluctantly following, his head bobbing up and down behind her. Perhaps something quite simple. She had spoken out to another human being. She had spoken out without wondering whether she would hurt some one else; she had unstopped the bitterness stopped up so long, and let it pour out on the ground like a libation. Far off now she could hear the whistling still, faint and far away. Then it stopped.

She and Ulysses were alone.

And in the silence, heat shimmering its invisible flames all around her, sky an immense blue radiance overhead, she saw what had really happened. Nicholas had not even tasted the bitterness; he had swallowed the hard exhilarating liquor of freedom instead. He had said, "I am proud of your mother." He had said, "I am proud of your brother." And it was as if she were being brought out at last from a dank, dark cell where all she could think of was suffering, and set on a high place with the sea below her.

"It is a good thing I found you, Ulysses," she said. What she meant was, that what had driven her toward him was the bondage of suffering, the endless chain of suffering, but stroking his nose, rubbing his ears, seeing slowly the soft curly hair grow back over the old wounds, she had felt life come back into her fingers. She had begun to live again.

CHAPTER 7

The better Ulysses felt, the more eagerly his soft lips nibbled and tasted at anything at all that came his way. Joanna was pleased to see that he was even sometimes admired by tourists who overran the village for a few hours at a time when one of the cruise ships stopped briefly at Santorini. It crossed her mind that someday perhaps a rich American would fall in love with Ulysses and offer him a permanent home. For the healthier and more beautiful he became, the more clearly Joanna faced that she could not be the guardian angel of a donkey once she got back to Athens and put on again the sober clothing of a dutiful daughter.

Her increasing pleasure in his velvety soft eyes was shot through with increasing anxiety. The precious month

[67

was drawing to a close; she had had her breath of freedom, of the heights where she and Nicholas and Ulysses
could stand together and look down like immortals on
the shining sea. And she had three or four paintings
strapped together to show Papa, who need never guess
what adventures other than these meditative ones she had
experienced.

Joanna was really a very practical person when it was
absolutely necessary that she be just that. So, during her
last week on the island, she was observed by the men
drinking ouzo in the café on the parapet, spending a great
deal of time on the terrace below, where the donkey-
drivers and their donkeys gathered after the climb, to wait
for those of their customers intrepid enough to risk the
climb down on the creaking saddles behind a pair of long
ears, down the steep hairpin curves of the track to the
port. Sometimes there was serious work to be had taking
down the empty casks of water, or wine, or barrels of
oranges to the freighters which kept Santorini alive.

And of course the great sport of the village, now the
season was on, was to stand along the parapet and make
jokes about the tourists. Fat, thin, old, young—they came
bumping up the sides of the precipice like grotesques, and
seemed a perpetual commentary on the human comedy,
their legs wide apart over the fat donkey backs, and sometimes bare beyond the confines of decency, their absurd
hats flopping, their faces flushed, their red mouths pursed
in terror, or giving an occasional small scream. There
were beautiful sedate young girls who could be made to

blush, and red-faced middle-aged men who glared about them to frown down any nonsense, any smile which might suggest that they looked as ridiculous as they actually were.

But Joanna, the village noticed, paid little attention to her traveling compatriots, the rich Athenians, or to the Americans off the cruise ships. She was to be found in the late afternoon, talking seriously with the donkey-drivers. There she stood, leaning casually against the parapet, her dark face glowing, her head thrown back sometimes in a laugh.

The old men shook their heads and winked. The arrogant Athenian was showing herself to be human after all. And which of the donkey men was she going to choose?

But down on the terrace below, Joanna would be asking innocent questions like, "What do you feed your donkey? Where does he sleep? How heavy a load can he carry?"

And the donkey-drivers teased her. "Oh, my donkey eats nothing but ice cream and gardenias."

"And mine drinks two glasses of ouzo to my one!"

The donkey-drivers considered her a harmless woman, a little mad about donkeys, and they teased her not unkindly about Ulysses. They were well aware that she was not interested in them. Or was she? The more observant among them became aware that she was often standing near Zarian, a particularly handsome young man with a black moustache and very white teeth. Sometimes she talked also to his donkey, one of the largest and healthiest of all. Zarian's donkey was an unusual beige color and his coat shone in the sun. He had a beautiful wooden saddle with a carved pommel and a bright blue blanket under it, and on his forehead a sunburst of fine beads and around his neck a blue necklace. Even his small hooves were kept clean of dung. She would stand with one arm casually around Ulysses' neck (Ulysses looked like a dwarf beside Zarian's huge beast) as if she were considering a very important matter, while Zarian, somewhat intoxicated by all the attention he was getting, boasted about how his donkey was the best of them all.

"I don't overload him. But he can carry more than most. See how straight his back is, compared to that poor crock over there!" Some of the donkeys looked moth-eaten; many had saddle sores, and many had swaybacks from carrying loads beyond their strength.

"I get back all and more than I spend in tips. People like a handsome donkey, eh Ulysses?" And he would bring out a lump of sugar from his pocket and tease Ulysses a little before holding out his hand flat and letting the eager lips take their prize.

"Well," he said one day, scratching his head and looking shyly out of his dark eyes like a fawn, "Why don't you come to the café and have an ouzo with me?"

This sally was greeted by guffaws of laughter and by a faint cheer. The drivers had been egging him on, no doubt.

Joanna nodded absent-mindedly. "Yes," she said, "a good idea. I have something I want to talk to you about."

The old men on the parapet sucked in through their moustaches and winked.

"She's too old for you, Zarian!" one called down when Joanna's long legs had disappeared among the maze of white houses at the top of the cliff.

"Old enough to be your mother!" another joined in.

Laughter and jeers broke out on all sides, and the donkeys, whose supper time it was, took up the sound and joined in with mocking brays.

"Come!" Zarian said curtly, to his donkey. He spat over the parapet as he left. The worst thing about Santorini is that there is simply no refuge from gossip. You can't turn around without a pack of fools laughing at you, or ask a stranger to share a glass without a vast comedy being made of it. Well, he had asked her and he was not going to be laughed out of it. It was simple courtesy, no more, he told himself, since she had bought his donkey ice cream more than once. And he remembered how she laughed when it disappeared, carton and all.

"There is no disposal problem on Santorini, I see!"

Nevertheless Zarian felt rather nervous when he sauntered down to the cafe later that evening in a clean white shirt, his Sunday shirt, as everyone in the cafe well knew.

"And what will you wear to church, Zarian?"

"Leave me alone," he glowered. "You're a bunch of island louts."

He could see Joanna walking down the street, alone. For once she had left Ulysses up at the chapel. She came toward him alone and frowning. There was an atmosphere of gloom about her, and it made him nervous.

"There you are," she said, but she did not smile. She

sat down and waited in silence while he ordered an ouzo for her. She ate an olive, lifted her glass, and met his eyes. But this was no flirtation, after all. She was in deadly earnest. And, he noticed, as he bent to light her cigarette, she was nervous. Her hand trembled so much, he had to use a second match.

"In a week I go back to Athens," she said.

(And what did that mean?)

She swallowed, and for just a wild instant he wondered if she was going to proposition him.

"The time is short," he answered with a smile meant to be reassuring. She might be old enough to be his mother but devil take her, she was handsome as she sat there, wrapped up in a solitude which still gave nothing.

She took another sip of ouzo. Should he make it easier for her?

"You are beautiful," he said, looking away.

"What?" The voice was harsh with surprise. "What are you talking about?"

"I said, 'you are beautiful'; that is what I am talking about." He stared at her boldly now. He did not care who was listening, for indeed the silence around them was tangible as a cloud.

Joanna threw back her head and laughed, a free laugh, a laugh of pure surprise with no malice in it. Then she turned to him, "You are too kind, dear Zarian." In a phrase she put distance between them. He had to admit that she was a lady, however eccentric a lady. And he called loudly for another ouzo.

"Listen, Zarian," she said almost tenderly, "I will give Ulysses to you, if you will take care of him." Before Zarian quite took in what this was all about, she went on, pleading with him now, "I know he is a small donkey. But he is very sweet and people admire him on the street. He makes a contrast with your noble donkey. Tourists will give you huge tips when they see the tiny Ulysses beside his huge brother. Oh please say you will take him!" Now she turned on him the full power of those dark eyes, in which anxiety and tenderness were equally matched—but not tenderness for him in his Sunday shirt with his black moustache. Not tenderness for his bright dark eyes.

Zarian's reaction was instantaneous. If she was going to give him a donkey, there must be some catch in it. After all, people don't go around giving away donkeys as if they were ice cream cones. His face, which had been so open, closed.

"Why give me a donkey?"

"Because, oh don't you see?" She made a gesture of mock despair, and it was her turn to make advances. "I can't take him with me to Athens. How would I feed him? Where would I put him? My father would turn me out of the house!" She smiled at Zarian with all the charm she could muster.

"But a donkey is worth money," Zarian said coldly. "Why don't you sell it then?"

Joanna looked crestfallen. "You can't sell what you love. Ulysses has become a friend." As soon as she uttered the words she felt how preposterous it was to think even of giving him away. How could she? She felt a lump in her throat rising up against all her sense of decorum, and to keep the tears from showing in her eyes, she said brusquely, "Why do you think I have been spending so much time down there?" she nodded toward the terrace below. "I have watched all the donkey-drivers to see how they treated their animals, and I have watched the donkeys themselves. You, Zarian," she said imperiously, "are the one who takes best care. Your donkey is the happiest and best-looking of them all."

The total shift in what had meant to Zarian a social occasion, an occasion of some importance, and an occasion which had cost him already the jeers and jokes of his peers, made him look stupid for the first time. The Athenian woman was making a fool of him, that was sure. And he made a motion to get up and leave, there and then. Joanna saw the flush of anger in his throat.

"No, sit down," she commanded. "You mustn't be angry with me. I am too helpless. You must be my friend. We will drink another ouzo—on me this time."

He was still standing. She pulled at his sleeve.

"Zarian—please."

It was he who felt helpless now. He stood, glaring around him, as if he would love to hit any one of the faces which had been drinking in every word, no doubt.

"Don't be a fool, Zarian," said an old voice from inside the cafe . . . whose it was Joanna didn't know. But she was hugely relieved to hear it speak like an oracle from the darkness, "She has made you an honest proposition."

The fact was that Zarian saw the uses of Ulysses, a perfect donkey for a frightened child off one of the boats. Tips would double. It was really, now that he came to face the reality of the situation, not a bad deal.

"All right," he said, sitting down again. And he called loudly for another ouzo. "Only I pay for the ouzo."

"Thank you," said Joanna who felt immensely relieved that the atmosphere of animosity and harshness was shifting in her favor. It had been, she thought, like one of those sudden squalls that rouse the Aegean to fury in a few moments.

"You are not cross, are you? I meant no harm."

And suddenly his frowning face broke up into a brilliant smile, and he laughed. He laughed and looked around him in triumph. He would go down in history as the driver to whom a woman gave a donkey. Such a thing had never happened before and would surely never happen again.

He lifted his glass and said, "It's a bargain. I take Ulysses," and drank. He seemed to Joanna to have grown larger in the last few seconds, to have become a giant. And as he grew larger over his bargain, she felt herself growing smaller and more miserable.

"What's the matter?" he asked, still laughing.

"I am sad," she said, leaning her face on one hand. "I am losing Ulysses, after all."

"He was a toy to you. A holiday toy," Zarian said coldly. "Now he will be useful, a working animal. It is more dignified."

And for that last word, Joanna forgave him much. For she had sensed all along that there was something offensive, in this village where everyone worked so hard, about an animal who did no work. Even the cats caught mice and rats. Only Ulysses had been exempt.

"I could never without him have reached the high places where I was able to go, because he carried my easel and painting things. He was not useless," she said, on the defensive. "And my holiday was a working holiday, too," she murmured.

"Painting?"

"Yes, you think that is not work?"

"Work pays for food, a bed. Work is what one has to do to live. Do you sell your paintings or do you give them away like donkeys?" He was serious. There was no sneer.

Joanna bowed her head. "Sometimes I give them away when I think they are good enough. Sometimes I give them away when a person says, 'Yes, that is the way it is. That is the way I see it too.' And although I earn my living in an office and that buys food for me and for my father, it is not real work."

"What is real work?"

"What one does for love, because one has to."

Zarian drank another sip of ouzo. He was enjoying himself. He had come through a risky passage, whole in his dignity. He had won in some way he could not quite define. The feeling made him expansive.

"My father was a fisherman. Drowned like all the others in this wicked sea." They looked down at the perfectly serene waters below, as gentle as silk. "He fished because he had to. That's what he always said. He liked the danger. Me," he smiled a mischievous smile, "I like solid ground under my feet. And," he glanced over at her humorously, "I like my donkey."

"You will be kind to Ulysses?" Joanna asked. She had held the question back until now, ashamed to expose her anxiety.

"Of course. A well-fed healthy donkey is good business."

"Well then," it was her turn to rise. She could not wait to get away. "I shall be taking the island boat next week. I'll leave him with you." It was an awkward moment. She fled, calling back, "Thank you, Zarian. I needed a drink!"

He sat for a time, receiving congratulations like someone who has just won in the lottery.

But Joanna walked up the hill alone, with a heavy heart, to lean her head against Ulysses in the dark and release the tears she had held back so long.

"At best we are two fools," she said to Ulysses. But, somehow, it was no comfort.

It was as if in this time of release from fear and the human burdens, Ulysses had become the symbol of her true life and of her joy . . . a sort of talisman. How would she ever be able to face her father and bring him to understand what had really been happening to her, without Ulysses? Ulysses, the perfect image of passive despair when she first saw him, and now, rich in his own new fur, wilful, free, Ulysses the perfect image of natural life?

[77

If it had not been for what Zarian said about the dignity of a work animal, she would never have been able to come to the decision. But she herself was going into exile. Life on the island, Ulysses, her painting—they would all become part of a dream, like her mother coming up the path with her hands full of anemones. And she herself, Joanna, was going back to prison alone. It was not like Joanna to weep for herself; she had not done so for years and years. But she wept now for the renascent self who must be buried again, and they were bitter tears.

CHAPTER 8

The last week flew, as last weeks are apt to do. . . . And Joanna found herself laying down her crayon or paint-brush only to look at Ulysses, comfortably cropping bits of dry grass and thyme, as if the end of their world were not imminent. She looked at him so intently that it seemed as if she were learning every hair, from his head to his funny tail which now wagged constantly to brush the flies off his gray flanks, from the healthy curly gray fur on his belly to his long sensitive ears, alert to her every move. She even tried to make some sketches of him, but gave up in despair. They looked like any donkey at all; it was clearly not possible to convey pictorially in just what this strange relationship had consisted. Being one of those who fully foresee every possible suffering and who experience

[81

it in advance, Joanna was cutting herself off from Ulysses. She looked at him already as one might look at something in the childhood past . . . as no longer part of her. He was over there in the sunny field, oblivious, contained in his animal life; and she was here beside her easel, struggling with her human one. Any intimacy had become too painful; she no longer rubbed her face against his soft nose. That belonged to the era of sentimental indulgences. They were about to enter, each in his own way, the era of hard reality.

Joanna thought about all this a good deal, as she climbed up to the heights. For she was well aware that she had arrived in Santorini like a starving person, starved, as she had thought, for the self she found as a painter, but starved also for another person altogether, whom Ulysses had brought to life again for the first time since the war. There is such a thing as animal comfort, she thought, after all. And in a world where one has had to witness too much suffering about which nothing could be done, there was the comfort of bringing back to life this one suffering beast, of making Ulysses well.

Far off she heard the melancholy whistle, and ran to the top of the hill to wave an answer to Nicholas. She waved and then ran down to the broken wall where they had sat and talked so often, and which she had painted so many times in the last weeks. When Nicholas appeared over the crest of the hill, she was busy with her box of canvases. Out of breath, he flung himself down beside her.

"They say you are leaving—is it true?" he asked when he had caught his breath.

"Yes," Joanna smiled, "but not today. You didn't need to run so fast!"

"Why are you going?" he asked.

"I have to get back to my father. It was to be only a month, you know, and we have had our month," she said, glancing over at Ulysses who was trotting up, his ears pricked, thinking no doubt that it must be lunch time and a ripe tomato would taste rather good after all those prickly weeds. "I go the day after tomorrow."

Nicholas did not answer.

"Look, I have olives and cheese, and ripe round tomatoes," she said. "Are you as hungry as I am?"

"I'm not hungry," said Nicholas, kicking the stubble with one foot.

"We can't let Ulysses have all this—he'll get much too fat!"

"Let him have it all," said Nicholas, without looking up.

Joanna let the silence fall. She respected it. The boy looked both lonely and dignified, standing there now with his head lifted as a sea gull sailed overhead. She pulled one of the canvases out of the painting box and turned it round in her hands.

"When I started to paint, you asked me why I did not paint the village. And I told you because I couldn't see it. Yesterday, perhaps because I am going, I felt suddenly that I must try to get it down, the steepness and

[83

the whiteness—the village like a bird's nest, so high over the sea." She held the painting to her chest. "I want to know your opinion." She turned it slowly round, still holding it against her.

Nicholas bent his head forward a little and looked at the painting with that intense look of curiosity with which he had so often looked at her, as if to take a nibble of her cheek. His eyes narrowed, and then he laughed his sudden laugh, shrill as a bird's cry.

"Why are you laughing?"

"I don't know. For pleasure," he frowned. "My opinion is that you have done well," he said seriously.

"It looks like your Santorini?" she pressed him. "People see things in different ways, you know. You don't have to say you like it."

"How do you speak to a painting?" he asked then. "How do you say yes to a painting?"

Joanna wanted terribly to hug him, standing there. But she knew that this would not do.

"I guess you just look at it," she said, "and see it."

"Yes," he said, his brilliant smile flashing out, "I see it." Then he laughed again, for pleasure.

"In that case, you may have it to keep," and she handed the small canvas to him.

Immediately he passed his dirty hands over it gently as if to feel what it was like, and he swallowed. "Mine," he said then, "to keep."

The slight pang Joanna felt when she handed it over melted away; it did seem to her one of her best paintings—and she had wanted to show it to her father—she could hear him saying in his dry ironic voice, "You would give the clothes off your back. If a bird needed it, you would give your soul to the bird. And you imagine perhaps that you are an angel, but how do you know you are not a fool?"

"Come," she said brusquely, "now let us eat."

Ulysses who had been waiting with his most long-suffering look, ears drooping, tail drooping, now pricked his ears and bent his soft nose down between them; they sat cross-legged facing each other, as they always had done.

"Here, you *have* been patient," Joanna said, giving Ulysses half a tomato.

Nicholas sat leaning one arm on the canvas with a proprietary air as if he feared a sea gull might swoop down and steal it from him. He looked up, narrowing his eyes.

"The birds are flying low. Storm. Perhaps you will not be able to go the day after tomorrow."

"But I've said goodbye," Joanna answered in a panic. "It is terrible to have to stay after one has said goodbye."

"Ulysses would be glad to stay. He has not said good-bye," he said, giving Ulysses a piece of cheese on his open hand.

"Ulysses is staying. I have given him to Zarian."

"Oh," the boy munched and considered this unexpected piece of news. "So I heard in the village. They say you are a fool."

"No doubt," Joanna said drily. "My father also says so rather often. I am quite used to being called a fool."

"And you don't mind?"

"Many people called my mother a fool, my father included," she said somberly. She sensed that the mood of the day was changing like the weather. She felt the wind tugging at her hair, a cool wind with a chill as of snow in it. "And what do you think, little Nicholas?" she asked, to break the dark mood.

"I think you are brave not to mind," he answered instantly. "I would mind."

"You are a man. Men cannot afford to be ridiculous." She said it to the wind as much as to the little boy beside her.

He was busy eating now, eating ravenously. He had discovered that, far from cutting his appetite, imminent parting had made him ravenously hungry; perhaps he did not hear anything but the sound of his own munching.

Joanna lay on her back, looking up at the blue sky in which high overhead mares' tails were flying, and she thought, I am drinking the sky. It is better and more intoxicating than wine. For she was now so low in cash that she had thought better of buying a last bottle of wine which she would not finish in any case. . . . After a while she pulled her hat down over her eyes.

When she opened them again and looked around, Ulysses was still standing there, finishing up the bread and cheese. But Nicholas and her painting had gone. Far down the hill he must be, for she heard his shrill melan-

choly whistle, in the distance. And for the second time
that morning she respected his dignity and his silence.

In her own mind, she had already skipped the next
day, a day which would be spent in not thinking and not
feeling, in packing up her valises, her easel, her painting
things, in making obeisance to the local gods—she paid a
formal call on the baker, on the druggist, on the man
who sold blue beads and hats for donkeys; she climbed the
hill to the chapel for the last time, and did not allow herself to embrace Ulysses. And, when the time came, after
a night of high wind which suddenly let down in the early
morning, she loaded the valises onto Ulysses' back. Let
him get used to his new life with the easy descent, loaded
with all she possessed. He would climb back, no doubt,
up the everlasting hairpin curves, heavy-laden, bearing
some tourist with cameras, bearing some fat rich old
woman.

And at last, for this leave-taking had become interminable indeed, they stood on the quay, waiting for the
island boat to put in. She tethered Ulysses, and walked up
and down, every now and then glancing upward, all the
steep way upwards to the terraces and square white houses
at the top. But when the boat came in, and the anchor
roared down, the pier, which had been as empty as a
stage set, was suddenly full of clamor and excitement.
The wind turned, as it were, and Joanna, who had been
looking back, was caught up in the elation of it all. She
ran to find Zarian, and on the way met Nicholas whose
small brown hand locked itself into hers without a word.

"Where is he?" she cried to the donkey men. "Where's Zarian?"

"Back there, looking for you"—and then she saw him, standing beside Ulysses, waving at her, and she ran back, terrified now of missing the big rowboat, already bobbing up and down at the quay.

"No time to say goodbye," she called back to the wind.

Her luggage had already been stowed.

"Keep an eye on Ulysses, Nicholas!" She wrenched herself away, not daring to look at him.

It was all happening much too fast, like an old film being run off at double speed. Although the wind had died down, the sea was still ruffled and the big rowboat struggled and reeled, so Joanna hung to the rail. There were ten yards or so between her and the pier when she lifted her head to wave once more to Zarian, to Nicholas, to Ulysses. "Oh my beastie!"

No one waved back. Nicholas and Zarian were trying to quiet Ulysses, and Ulysses was struggling with all his strength to break the tethering rope. He was straining forward, shaking his head from side to side in an odd, insistent, heart-breaking rhythm. As the boat got further and further away, this rhythm increased in intensity. And finally he lifted his head and uttered a piercing bray.

At that moment all Joanna's wise decisions exploded in an immediate, irrational emotion which she could not control. She staggered over to the rowing man, quite oblivious of the fact that she was rocking everyone and had knocked over a woman's bundle. "Will they take a donkey on board?" she shouted.

"What?" the man muttered, busy with his oars, and just now pulling hard to bring the boat about to the ship's ladder.

"Donkey!" shouted Joanna, beside herself.

"Ask the officer," the man said. Joanna stood in the boat and waited till the other passengers had been helped up onto the slippery platform projecting from the ship. Then she called across to the officer in his immaculate whites, "Can I bring my donkey aboard?"

He peered down at her eager face, and grinned. "Is it a joke?"

"No," Joanna stamped her foot. "It's not a joke!"

He shook his head. "No donkeys on this ship, lady. You'll have to wait for the freighter, two days from now." She turned back and saw that Ulysses had somehow managed to pull Zarian and Nicholas to the pier's edge, and there he stood, dumb with misery, shaking his head back and forth again.

"I'm going back," she said to the boatman, in a rather severe voice, as if to say, it is perfectly natural to wish to go back. After all, I cannot leave my donkey. I am absolutely sane and in my right mind. "Please." But the please came out high and quavery.

The boatman took his time. He had lit a cigarette and was resting on his oars.

"No hurry," he said gently. "The donkey will wait."

"He might hurl himself into the sea—try to swim—"

"Don't fool yourself. A donkey's a canny beast."

Joanna waved, and made signs to explain what was happening, but of course it was too preposterous to be believable, and when the rowboat was within a few feet of the pier, Zarian called out, "What have you forgotten?"

"Nothing," she shouted. "I'm not going."

Nicholas leapt into the air and did a little dance. His face was full of mischief. "She's not going!" he shouted to the sea gulls. "She's not going!" he turned and whispered into Ulysses' ear.

Zarian spat.

His eyes narrowed as she ran toward them and flung her arms around Ulysses' neck and rubbed her head against his nose. "I'm not going to leave you. I'm taking you with me," she told him. "The freighter will take us both the day after tomorrow," she explained to Zarian. "It's all right."

"All right for him," Zarian said, sardonically. Joanna was kneeling beside Ulysses, one arm around his neck; she looked up without a trace of compunction.

"I'm sorry," but it was clear that she was not sorry at all, that she was bursting with happiness.

"All right for you, but you have made me a laughing-stock. Wait till the drivers hear this!" And he nodded his head toward the hairpin road up the cliff, where a stream of donkeys was plodding its way, heads bobbing up and down, carrying casks of wine and cases of canned goods, and a fat old gentleman in a panama hat, with a black umbrella open over his head.

"Yes," Nicholas looked at her anxiously, "it is serious. You said, up there, a man cannot stand it—being ridiculous," he enunciated each syllable as if the word were a precious object she had given him.

Joanna rose to her feet.

Zarian faced her and he was angry. "First you flirt with me and get me to invite you to an ouzo; you drink three ouzos and then you tell me what all this is about. It is not me you are flirting with, it's a donkey! They were laughing at me up there in the cafe, you heard them. So you give me the donkey—and I've heard nothing since then but sly jokes 'what did you give her in exchange, eh Zarian?' " (his voice grew shrill as he imitated the gossips of the village) "and *now*," he spat again, "now you take back the donkey! What am I supposed to do? Jump into the sea?"

"We have got to consider the whole thing very quietly," Joanna answered, looking down because she was afraid she would burst out laughing. "You could tell them that I am out of my mind," she offered tentatively.

"They know that already," Zarian said coldly. "That is no news."

Nicholas was pulling gently at her sleeve. She bent down and he whispered something in her ear. She nodded absent-mindedly. After all, why not?

"And what if I gave you something instead of Ulysses?"

Zarian narrowed his eyes. "What, for instance?"

"The freighter doesn't come for two days. Is that right?

Well then, I will paint something for you. I will paint the village, or your house . . ."

Zarian scratched his head. A wily look came into his eyes. There is nothing more pleasant to a Greek than a bargain, but he wants to make the terms himself. Therein lies the genius of the bargainer. He carefully put out his cigarette, crushing it under the heel of his boot. "No," he said, but he could not keep the smile of triumph out of his eyes.

"What then?"

"My donkey? Will you paint my donkey, eh? The drivers may laugh then if they please, but they will envy me."

"Ah," said Joanna, "you see?" And she laid a hand on Nicholas' head, as if to acknowledge that of them all he was the clever one, as indeed he was.

CHAPTER 9

The second departure two days later felt like a holiday instead of the end of a holiday. It seemed as if half the village had decided to come down to watch The Embarkment of Joanna and Ulysses, and Ulysses was resplendent in a new hat, with a red poppy on it. This time it was late afternoon; the men in the cafes had come down to the pier, some of them, and waved and shouted and laughed, until Joanna in her gypsy pants and Ulysses in his hat disappeared into the hold.

Zarian was already lording it over the other drivers, and carried the small painting of his donkey down with him to the pier. Every now and then he took it out and looked at it with a very painterly expression, holding it at arm's length and screwing up his eyes. If anyone happened to come up behind him to see what he was looking at, he was very happy indeed to point out how well Joanna had captured his donkey's expression, and how exactly she had painted the blue beads around his neck and his small elegant hooves. But Nicholas' sharp eyes had seen at once that this was a different sort of gift from the one that now hung in his bedroom, and which he was considering giving to the school, so that it could be admired and seen by more people.

"For Zarian you painted what he can see; but for me you painted what *you* see," he had told Joanna. They all felt freed of some constraint now that Ulysses was going to Athens. Joanna hugged Nicholas so hard that she thought his ribs might crack.

But when the freighter had rounded the dead volcano island, coal-black in the evening light, Nicholas and Zarian climbed back the steep winding road and did not say anything. Every now and then they stopped, in a silent accord, and leaned on the wall and looked down; the whole scene was bathed in a rosy light as the sun set. It was peaceful, but empty. Very far away they could see the smoke of the freighter.

"Well," said Nicholas, "she's gone now, but she came." He bit his lip.

Meanwhile Joanna, who had not thought further than getting Ulysses safely aboard, was standing in the prow despite the sudden cold wind. Sufficient unto the day is the anxiety thereof—she had to admit that she had made no plans whatsoever as to what to do when they landed

at Piraeus, twelve miles from Athens. It would be nine
o'clock; she had spent all but a few drachmas, and even
if Ulysses could walk those twelve miles carrying the
luggage, she herself certainly could not.

These reflections were interrupted by a sailor who
came to say that a woman in the stern wanted to speak
to her.

Joanna found a peasant woman, dressed in black, standing beside what had been two gardenia plants (she remembered seeing them tenderly carried on at Santorini).
They had been eaten down to the root by Ulysses, standing beside them with his most innocent expression. His
velvety eye turned toward Joanna as she approached with
a look as if to thank her for a specially elegant supper. But
Joanna was too absorbed in the angry laments of the
woman to give him more than a passing gentle slap on his
nose.

"The dirty brute has destroyed my flowers—which I am
taking to my widowed daughter, which I have tended
and nourished and watered!" Grief had not made her
speechless.

"Oh dear," Joanna said, "it is awful, but I have spent
all my money. What can I do? Look, if you will give me
your address, I will replace the gardenias—I really will."

It seemed a bad augury as the beginning of Ulysses'
life as a civilized city donkey. Joanna felt as ruffled and
upset as a cat whose fur has been rubbed the wrong way.

She felt no better when the freighter entered the port,
and she realized what an idyllic life she had been lead-

[97

ing. Now she saw the hundreds of ships in their berths, the elegant yacht-like *Delos* at anchor and all lit up, as it lay there waiting for a cargo of rich tourists. She saw the terminus buildings, the ships, the cafes, the hundreds of automobiles—and then she looked at Ulysses, such a small, vulnerable donkey, so ill-suited to city life, so omnivorous too! And for a moment she almost agreed with her father's opinion that she was a born fool and no doubt about it.

Then she remembered a friend of hers who had a shop selling fishermen's goods. It could not be too far from the quays, and perhaps he would take them in for the night.

It was nearly ten when Joanna and Ulysses reached the shop, but thank goodness there was still a light to be seen in the back room where Christopher did his accounts and sometimes slept. In answer to the knock, he came sleepily out, yawning, but when he saw the strange pair— Ulysses under a forest of easel and valises, and Joanna in her gypsy pants, looking for once rather meek—he burst out laughing.

"Whatever are you doing here, Joanna?" he sked. "And with a donkey!"

Christopher looked very tall and very thin above her, laughing with surprise and pleasure. He resembled one of the Picasso clowns of the blue period, and looked a little like a donkey himself, he had such a long face. It was this air of innocence and surprise that had made him such a good agent during the war. Here in Piraeus he had been one of the strongest links in the chain when they were helping prisoners to escape. And because he had hardly seen Joanna since those days, he thought of her still as almost a child.

When she had explained, in a single sentence that went on for several minutes, that she had to find a place to sleep and then the next day someone with a truck or cart who could get Ulysses and herself into Athens while her father was at his office, so she could hide the donkey in the cellar. . . . She stopped when she ran out of breath. "You see, Christopher?"

"I see nothing whatever. Why this donkey?"

Joanna promised to tell him the whole story, but first, could they come in?

"Well," Christopher looked dubious. "Not here. Your donkey would spend the night eating my new stock of straw hats. You know, Joanna," and he twinkled with amusement, "it is one thing to hide an English soldier and quite another to hide a donkey!" And he chuckled. "Hiding a donkey is like trying to hide a compulsive child and a crazy person all at once."

"Oh dear," said Joanna. He was quite right, of course.

"I'll think of something, just let me get my jacket."

When he came back, he was full of ingenious plans. They went first to the wood-seller three doors down. And there in the sweet smelling shop, Ulysses was relieved of his burdens and tethered to a post, and given half a loaf of bread for his supper.

Then Christopher took Joanna out to a restaurant near

[99

the pier and made her eat a big dish of *mousaka* and drink some coffee while she told him the whole story. But it was not really the story of Ulysses; it was the story of herself in the last month. This was different from talking with Nicholas; this was talking to an adult. This was different from talking to a donkey, it was talking to a human being, to an equal, for in Christopher too she recognized the wildness, the anarchic angel, even though he had found his freedom by leading the very simplest possible of lives. Well, perhaps that was why she could talk to him as she did.

What she told him was that she perhaps would never be a great painter, "No Cézanne," she said with a smile. But she told him that she had learned on Santorini, "and with Ulysses' help," that she must never again resign herself. "It's that, you see, that terrible resignation which I caught from my father like a fungus. I will never again live from day to day, just to keep time passing, never again!" she said, and her eyes flashed.

"This has been a long time in coming," Christopher said, "but you are right, of course. And if it took a sick donkey to bring you to your senses, well, so much the better!"

"To bring me to my senses . . ." Joanna mused. "Yes. Oh Christopher, how wonderful it is to be able to talk to someone!"

"You mean to tell me," he teased, "that you have been silent for a month, you who have not stopped to draw breath, since you arrived in Piraeus!"

"I talked to a little boy," she answered, "and to a donkey-driver . . . but, you see, I seemed so strange to them. I was as strange there as Ulysses is here." And she leaned her chin on her hand, feeling suddenly too tired to say another word. For she saw with absolute clarity that there was really no place where both she and Ulysses could be at home together. And she wondered if it had been a fatal mistake to bring him with her. But if one can't trust a compelling instinct such as that, what can one trust?

"Just a minute," Christopher said. He had seen a burly man come in and sit down at a table outside. "We are in luck!"

And when he came back, after conferring for some time with the man, their two heads close together like conspirators, Christopher was chuckling with amusement and delight. "Heaven protects the fool," he said. "That man is a trucker—and he has to go into Athens tomorrow morning, early, on a job; he'll take you and Ulysses in for nothing—"

"Oh how kind of him! Why ever should he?" Joanna said.

"Well, he knows something about what we were doing in the war. I did him a good turn once myself." He looked at her quizzically. "You know there is some advantage in being poor. The poor help each other. If you had been able to pay, my guess is that my friend would have refused to be bothered."

"I like to be independent," Joanna said quietly.

"Yes," Christopher was suddenly serious. The gentle mocking tone had left him. "You used to be rich. When you are poor, you learn that independence is an illusion."

"Do you?"

"You're such a funny mixture of innocence, courage, of youngness and oldness, Joanna, you are a puzzle!"

"I have lived so long in the dark with my father," she said, "I am easily dazzled."

Christopher listened. It was one of his charms that he listened. He did not rush in to deny what was obviously true, nor to comfort where comfort would be only words.

"You know, sometimes on Santorini, the light made me feel quite crazy, drunk . . . it is impossible to paint. You would have to break the spectrum. So I ended by painting stones and small starved tufts of flowers."

"Yes, I can understand that."

"But what was wonderful there was to live so close to the marrow. This is the first hot meal I've had in ages. I've been living on bread, tomatoes, and cheese."

"And what happens when you live close to the marrow?"

"What happens?" Joanna looked up, startled. "First, loneliness." She laughed, "Of course I had Ulysses; without Ulysses I should have been very lonely. He was the ideal companion, not quite human—"

"But almost?" Christopher smiled tenderly.

"Yes, almost. It is comforting to rub one's face on his soft nose, but he does not penetrate to where the hard questions lie. One is still quite alone with him, alone . . . yet comforted."

"And after loneliness . . . for loneliness is only the

medium, or the passage to somewhere else . . . am I right?"

"How do you know so much, Christopher?" It was her turn to tease. "Is this what one learns about life selling fishermen's hats?"

"Well, why not?" Christopher suddenly laughed. "It's a free sort of life in a way. To be such a failure, I mean. But you haven't answered my question!"

She watched him light a little thin cigar, and blow the thick blue smoke slowly into a ring and then another ring like a magician.

"All I know is that at the office I am never myself. I wear a mask all the time at home. I wear a mask for my father. On the island I was so much myself that I did not even need to think what being myself means."

"A painter?"

"Oh Christopher, you know I'll never be a real painter, but it is a way of seeing things, the essence of things— their shapes, their textures, what makes them real. I suppose that for me it's the opposite of day-dreaming." She stopped and closed her eyes. "The island is a state of mind. I thought I wanted to talk about it, but I find I don't."

"Keep your secret," Christopher said, "and I'll take you back now to the shop. You can sleep on my cot there and I'll go to a friend's."

"Yes," she said, "I am suddenly tired. And grateful, dear Christopher! Whatever would I have done without you?"

Christopher gave her a slow look out of his dark eyes. And puffed another ring. "I have an idea your guardian angel would have made other arrangements."

[103

Joanna and Ulysses

CHAPTER 10

With Ulysses and a bale of
hay safely stowed away in
the cellar, and an hour still to go before her father was
due home for lunch, Joanna felt that she did indeed have
a guardian angel, although her heart was beating uncom-
fortably fast, and she knew that the truck driver had been
quite right to roar with laughter.

"You imagine you can hide this animal in the cellar?
Hide him indefinitely?"

"Well," she had said, "perhaps not indefinitely . . ."

For as soon as she had entered the house, she had
sensed that this was more than just hiding a donkey from
her father, that in fact what she was doing was trying to
bring together two parts of herself. And here, taking out
a clean dress, walking on a soft red carpet in her room,

[105

smelling the roses her father had left on her bureau, taking the photograph of her mother down in its heavy silver frame to look at it closely, she was already quite a different person from the one who had stood in the prow of the boat only a month ago, thinking, "Listen sky, listen gulls, I am Joanna!"

Ulysses, a prisoner down there in the cellar, was the part of herself who would soon be buried, too. She was expected at the office the next day . . . and what then? She brushed her hair hard, then stopped to listen in the middle of a stroke. Not a sound. At least for the present Ulysses was perfectly quiet.

After that, she wandered about the house, dusting furniture, shaking out the rugs and opening all the windows to let out the stale smell of pipe tobacco. She had already begun to be caught in the coil of daily life, begun to run instead of walk, with no time to do more than cock an ear down towards the cellar now and then. Passing the big gilt-framed mirror in the hall with a duster in her hand, Joanna caught a glimpse of herself, her hair pulled back with a barrette, her face tense.

"So, you are back again," she addressed the old Joanna.

She sat down then and lit a cigarette, the strapped-together canvases at her feet, sat there in the middle of nowhere, afraid to undo the straps, for how would her strange austere paintings look here? As incongruous as a donkey in the parlor? She did not have the courage to find out. And instead darted into the kitchen to set rice to boil, to put eggs to bake in the oven, slice tomatoes, her fingers automatically deft at these familiar tasks, like a machine that had been allowed to run down and now was wound up tight again.

When it all was ready—roses in the center of the table, water poured in two tall glasses, and a bottle of dry sherry on a little tray in the parlor (her father detested ouzo, said it was a drink for truck drivers)—she took a deep breath and ran down the dark stairs to the cellar and threw her arms around Ulysses, who was standing in his improvised stall, a rope tied around a pipe to hold him fast, like patience itself. Joanna could see his dark eye turned toward her. "Oh dear," she sighed. "Whatever is going to happen to us, Ulysses?"

Just then, she heard her father's key in the lock.

"Joanna, where are you?" he called in the impatient tone of a child who expects someone to be there at the door when he comes back from school.

"Here, Papa!" she called back, racing up the stairs and closing the door behind her, leaning against it a moment to catch her breath. Did she hear a faint whiffle below?

"Come here, let me look at my girl!" He laid down his briefcase, his panama hat, and his stick in the meticulous order with which he regulated all things, and she ran to embrace him. How small he seemed, how frail— the light suit hung on him, too loosely.

"You haven't been eating enough," she scolded. "You have lost weight, Papa."

"I have been lonely," he said. "That woman is not as good a cook as you are, and then she sometimes couldn't come, one of the children has been ill." He launched into a long tale of all the minute happenings of the past weeks; they stood there in the hall while it all poured out, and Joanna felt too much respect to interrupt. But finally, slipping an arm through his, she said,

"Come, Papa. I have sherry in the parlor. We'll celebrate with an apéritif!"

It was her turn to talk, as she poured out two small glasses. "Now you are here, I'm home," she said. "The house felt so queer when I got back—such a smell of stale tobacco! So sad and closed! But now you are here, Papa . . ."

"Well, you see how it is!"

"Yes, I do see." But what she saw at the back of her eyes was the high field and Nicholas running toward her shouting his joy.

"So," her father sipped his sherry, and gave a small smile. "It was good on your primitive island? It was what you wanted?"

"Too much what I wanted," she threw him a smile as she disappeared into the kitchen.

"It suits you," her father nodded. "You look like a gypsy, but it suits you very well."

Joanna felt she was sitting down to eat lunch with a stranger, but whether the stranger was herself, her old self, or her Papa, looking so old and frail and tired, she could not decide. She watched him eat with evident pleasure, his hands trembling a little. But she herself could not swallow. She was much too anxious, with half her being nothing but an ear turned towards the total silence of the cellar.

"We'll look at the paintings tonight," her father said. She knew that all he wanted now was to lie down in the cool and dark, the newspaper open unread on his knees, and the panama hat pulled down over his face.

It was her real life coming back again, a life in which just keeping alive took all one's time and energy and the important things got put off, always put off. It was foolish, but Joanna felt close to tears, as she lay down herself, feeling the cool pillow against her cheek. Fortunately her father had not seemed curious to know why she had spent the night at Christopher's shop, had hardly listened to her elaborate explanations. He was frankly not interested. Now she was home, he wanted her as she had been, the thread of their companionship resumed unbroken exactly as it had always been, and as it would always be as long as he lived.

But just as Joanna dozed off, the house shook with a tremendously loud bray . . . Joanna had forgotten what an unholy sound it is, and after all on Santorini there was space for it to echo in. She leaped from her bed, hearing her father shout.

When she reached him, he was sitting up, trembling with rage. "I'll sue them! I'll get a lawyer!"

"Papa! Papa! What are you talking about? You have had a bad dream." Joanna laid a cool hand on his forehead, but he brushed it away impatiently.

"Didn't you hear that donkey? It's certainly Deme-

[109

trios—they got rid of their horse because I complained of the noise, but this is his revenge! A donkey!"

Demetrios was the next-door neighbor; his horse had stamped and whinnied early in the morning. And while she was away, her father had somehow intimidated poor Demetrios into housing the horse down the street.

"You imagined it," Joanna lied without a qualm. "I heard no donkey."

"One could not dream such a sound, my dear girl! Unless one was ready for a madhouse."

At this moment Joanna had to go into the next room to stifle an acute fit of giggles. It was a pure nervous reaction, for she was in a panic.

However, now he was thoroughly awake, her father decided to go back to the office and to do an errand on the way. Oh, what a relief it was when she heard the door close behind him! But then she walked up and down holding her head in her hands. The time was limited, and sooner or later she would be found out. And what then? Anyway it was clear that she was entirely unsuited to leading a double life.

For the first time Joanna almost wished she had left Ulysses behind on Santorini. Being shut up in a cellar was no life for him, and she herself found the tension excruciating. She got scolded at the office for being absentminded, and at home she was far too nervous to rest. There is no problem that has not some solution, she admonished herself. It was preposterous that she, who had not hesitated to take on a dying donkey, was now completely baffled by what was to be done with him! And he did loom so very large, as if, she sometimes thought, the real Joanna whom she had kept secret for so long had now assumed a visible shape—she had to laugh, for it seemed appropriate that this shape should be that of a donkey! Yet perhaps for the very reason that Ulysses had become the symbol of her other self, she found it impossible to tell her father and be done with it, once and for all. She was frightened not only of his anger, and impatience with what would seem to him the purest folly of course, but she was also afraid that if she had to render Ulysses up, she would, so to speak, be giving up the living part of herself which had begun to paint again.

"Mama, what would you do?" she asked the photograph, and the smiling open face had only one answer to give, "Make a clean breast of it, my child!" Oh her mother had always been as clear as daylight, and Joanna was aware that she herself had inherited from her father complexities and subtleties which inhibited action. We should never have been left alone together, we two, she thought in her gloom. She saw clearly how they had lived side by side all these last years, sealed off in their private worlds, only pretending to connect. It had all been like a game, she playing the part of nurse to a neurotic old man, he playing the part (perhaps) of a neurotic old man who allows himself to be nursed. It had gone on so long, the stifling, the routine of pretence, how could it end now? Let in daylight now? And because she felt caught in an

[111

ignoble coil, Joanna began to be impatient with her father's foibles.

"You can finish the paper later, Papa. Supper is ready," she said sharply, and caught his surprised hurt look as he laid the paper down.

"Is there really any reason for hurry?" he said, his mouth trembling a little. "Are you going out?"

"No, of course not. Do I ever go out?" The tone was openly cross, and Joanna blushed with shame when her father answered gently.

"It would do you good to go out. You haven't seen Uncle Alexis since your return."

But how could she go out and leave her father alone with the secret part of herself in the cellar?

"I'm too tired," she answered, closing her face against him.

And three days later she broke one of the best dishes.

"Butter fingers!" her father said, not unkindly. "You are nervous, my dear!"

Joanna burst into tears. That, too, was unlike her; she had to invent a reason for such violent behavior.

"You're all upset." Her father looked concerned, then smiled indulgently while she knelt on the floor awkwardly picking up the pieces of broken china. "If I didn't know you so well, I'd say you were in love!"

Joanna's hands flew to her cheeks and she bowed her head, "No—no—Papa—but," she invented, "you still haven't seen my paintings."

"Well, well," he said, beginning to bustle about, "we'll

look at your paintings right now. We'll make it a cere-
mony. Coffee, brandy."

Now she was in for it, Joanna did not want to open
the strapped canvases. She was afraid to. She was afraid
that here, in this other world, all she had done would
seem unreal. What did it matter, anyway, she told herself? She had no pretensions. She did not take her painting
seriously.

She set the five canvases up against chairs and tables
in the parlor, one by one, and then she and her father
sat down with their coffee, and there was a long painful
silence.

Although Joanna was looking straight at what she had
done, she could not see it at all. They might have been
pieces of cardboard, blank as faces with closed eyes.
Why was her father so silent? He was leaning his chin
on his cane and he was looking very intently at whatever
it was he saw.

"Well, Papa?" Joanna murmured when she could stand
it no longer.

"Look!" He nodded his head toward one of her early
paintings, a rather pretty watercolor of a corner of a
monastery, bright blue shutters against white walls and
window boxes full of petunias and roses.

"And now look!" he pointed with his stick to the first
of the paintings of the stone wall on Santorini. "I am silent
because I am so astonished. You have become a painter,
Joanna, a serious one," he said gravely. "You have grown
up."

Joanna shut her eyes. "Do you really think so? Is it true?" Her father, she realized, had never before taken her seriously. He had indulged her in her whims, as she indulged him. This was different.

"Yes," she answered then, "on Santorini I became a different person."

"Bravo!" her father said, as he turned his head from one to the other of the canvases, "Bravo!"

Joanna was taken wholly by surprise. She had been so busy being anxious that she had almost forgotten the paintings; and when she set them up for her father, she had been too self-conscious to look at them herself. But that "Bravo!" uttered with such energy, with such conviction, shocked her back to seeing. Was it true? Here in the dark room, cluttered with small objects, the paintings looked strangely clear and naked, so very simple, after all, she thought . . . and yet . . . and yet . . . for just a second she breathed the air of Santorini where she had been intimately related to stones and tufts of grass and to an immensely high blue sky, and to wind, and to a donkey. . . . "Ulysses," Joanna murmured. It was a fact that she had in the last hour forgotten all about him.

"What about Ulysses?" her father asked.

"Nothing, Papa, I was just thinking about journeys—"

"Well, there is just time for a little siesta," her father said, "a half hour anyway." He put his feet up and pulled the panama hat down over his eyes. "You have made me happy," he murmured, as she kissed him, and pulled up a steamer rug over his knees, "happier than I have been for a long time . . ."

Then Joanna tip-toed out and crept down the stairs to tell Ulysses, to give him some fresh hay to munch, and to be sure his pail of water was full. His soft nose nuzzled against her and she scratched his head between his ears, and then stroked his nose and felt the curly soft fur under his belly, all the time whispering endearments. Then she crept upstairs, leaving the door open (she must be sure to remember to close it when her father woke)— and went to her room to shut her eyes and think.

Perhaps it was the relief she experienced because her father had so unexpectedly rallied to the Santorini paintings; or perhaps the anxiety of the last days had taken a toll. Anyway she fell asleep five minutes after she had invoked whatever guardian angels might be around to help her imagine what to do about Ulysses.

She was roused out of deep sleep by a loud cry, cursing, and a clatter of hooves.

"Joanna! Joanna! Help!"

When she dashed into the parlor, her father was sitting up, fanning himself with what remained of his panama hat, and Ulysses was peering in through the door with a rather wild look in his eye.

"Am I stark raving mad, or is that animal standing there glaring at me a donkey?"

"Oh Papa, what has happened to your hat?"

"When I opened my eyes, I heard munching and looked

up into a donkey's face—a donkey standing there over me eating my hat!"

"Oh Papa!" Joanna could not help laughing and now she had started, she couldn't stop. "Oh Ulysses!" She ran and put an arm around him and stood there, with tears of laughter pouring down her cheeks. "I'm sorry, Papa, but you must admit it is rather funny!"

"Funny?" Her father was red in the face, a bad sign. "Funny? To wake under a donkey's open mouth, to find my panama torn to shreds! Funny, eh?"

"Forgive me, Papa," she implored. "I brought him from Santorini—it is a long sad story."

"No doubt. But I don't want to hear it. You get that animal out of here before I come back from work this evening!" said her father, automatically putting the chewed remnants of his hat on his head, picking up his briefcase and stick, and about to dash out of the house like a man pursued by the furies. "I mean it!"

Joanna said a prayer not to laugh, for she was in a fit of hysterical giggles. But nothing did any good—she fell into a chair, hiccuping, and Ulysses followed her into the parlor and stood behind her, his head drooping over her shoulder.

"You are a clever beastie to have chewed off your rope—"

"Clever?" Her father was beside himself. "He's a dolt like all donkeys. I will not have a donkey in my house!"

"Papa, please don't be cross!" Joanna wiped the tears of laughter from her eyes. "He was in a terrible state, dying, and I saved him. Don't you see, I couldn't help it!"

"Other people *can* help saving any sick donkey they happen to see! I expect to find him gone when I get back. Do you understand?"

"Yes, Papa."

And the door banged shut.

"Oh Ulysses," Joanna sighed. "Oh Ulysses!"

Ulysses gave a short whiffling sound, as if he felt relieved himself that the wild man, who had been shouting so, had at last left them in peace.

"And Papa has gone out in half his hat, looking quite out of his mind," again she began to giggle in spite of herself. She could imagine the tale he would tell in the office; at last the full implications of her situation sank in. It was not a moment for laughing.

The first question was whether Ulysses, who had apparently climbed the stairs with no trouble at all, could be persuaded to go down them. She looked at her watch—she was ten minutes late already! But she couldn't leave. There was nothing to be done but telephone, say she was ill, stay home and try to solve the problem.

Ulysses balked at the top of the stairs—it was not so much, she divined, that he couldn't go down, as that he didn't want to. But when Joanna ran down the stairs with a half loaf of bread and two tomatoes, Ulysses pricked his ears and after a decent interval which donkey-pride required, came trotting down with a great clatter of hooves, and allowed himself to be tied up again.

"One thing can be said for you, my beastie, you are not, by the grace of God, a balky donkey." And he really was handsome, a handsome fellow, she thought, watching him gulp down a tomato. She felt a little hurt that her father had not seen what a particularly charming donkey he was, but perhaps in time he would come to see.

An hour later, the telephone rang, and Joanna heard her father saying "I'll give you a week, Joanna. I realize that I have been unreasonable, but within a week, that creature has to be disposed of."

"Thank you, Papa. Oh, thank you!" But when Joanna put down the receiver she thought that in an impossible dilemma neither a week nor even a month is really any help. The panic, the giggles, and the long childish dream were over, and now she had to come to terms with reality.

It was out of the question to sell Ulysses into bondage; or even to give him to just any donkey-driver who would overwork him and never buy him a decent hat! No! Joanna said to herself. After all, that was what she had learned on Santorini when she had made the supreme effort to behave like a reasonable human being. Very well, she said to herself with a bravado she could not quite believe in, reality, but reality on my own terms.

Let us apply logic, she told herself. In the first place, Ulysses is beautiful and charming. To whom would this charm appeal? Secondly, his is truly a fine story, full of pathos and drama. To whom would such a story appeal? As a poem begins as a musical stir, as a precise image which bursts into music, so for no reason at all, Joanna had the image in her mind of Mykonos and of Flavia, who ended her infrequent letters with the words, "Tell me your life and miracles." Flavia had some Spanish blood and this phrase was apparently a Spanish form of address, or so Joanna vaguely remembered. And then, the whole, the beautiful, the only solution shimmered before her eyes, no mirage, but a perfect design like a poem. In the first place, the island of Mykonos is fashionable. Tourists pour out into its labyrinthine white streets two or three times a week; every boat stops there, and the semi-circle of houses along the beach has become one great bazaar. Secondly, Mykonos has become a center for fine weaving, and Flavia herself was valiantly at work in a small studio of local weavers in one of the white houses. Joanna closed her eyes; she could see Ulysses in a sumptuous hat, brushed and shining, his hooves kept as clean as Zarian's donkey's, walking with his delicate steps down the pier, bells on his headband, blue beads round his neck—and a whole collection of woven bags and blankets in his saddle bags and on his back! A sure-fire lure for the tourists as they tumbled out of the boats looking for local color. And without a moment's doubt, Joanna sat down and wrote "Dear Flavia, I will tell you my life and miracles. . . . You will see that the miracles concern you."

Before the week was out, Flavia, coerced into taking part in someone else's miracle, had written a grudging acceptance of Ulysses. "Of course," she added, "your idea about using the donkey to sell weaving is utterly romantic and ridiculous. When, dear Joanna, will you learn to distinguish between fact and fantasy?"

Joanna read the letter, half-smiling and half-frowning.

[119

Evidently it had reached Flavia on one of the days when the Spanish blood, of which she was so proud, had been forgotten, and she had become a terribly matter-of-fact Greek. But at least Ulysses had a definite destination at last. And he would surely be happy on Mykonos, where there were no automobiles to frighten him, where life still could be lived at a donkey's pace, and where he would find plenty of others of his own kind.

That night she and her father sat drinking coffee from the best white and gold cups which were brought out for special occasions. He had read Flavia's letter over; nodding his head, and then let it fall with an absent-mindedness very unlike him, and looked across at his daughter with a slightly quizzical expression.

"Perhaps it is time, Joanna, that you did learn to distinguish fact from fantasy."

Joanna was in no mood to be scolded; the mask of dutiful daughterliness closed down over her face; she folded her hands in her lap, and prepared to listen to one of her father's not infrequent philosophical explorations of what he imagined her character to be. She had missed the twinkle in his eye. Perhaps she had been too concerned about Ulysses to realize that in some subtle way her relation to her father had been changing since her return from Santorini. But he himself was aware of it. He had had time to come slowly, by his own ways (never simple, always complex and even devious) to a new understanding. For days now he had boasted to his cronies in the square, "You know, Joanna has become an artist. It is quite extraordinary. Here I have lived with this girl for thirty years and I never suspected that she had serious work in her! Astonishing . . ." So that he had by now come to take for granted what Joanna herself was totally unprepared to hear.

"Yes, Papa," she said, and bent her head.

"It is pure fantasy to imagine that you were cut out to be a drudge, a housekeeper, a filing clerk or whatever you imagine you are."

Joanna lifted her eyes and perhaps for the first time in their long acquaintance looked at her father as one human being to another.

"The fact is," he said, smiling now, "that you are an artist. *That* is the fact we have to reckon with."

Joanna felt a great surge of hope rise, only to be followed by the inevitable wave of self-doubt.

"But how can one *know*, Papa?" She realized that as long as she had immolated herself in being a good daughter, she had been able to escape coming to terms with the real Joanna; she felt terrified. It was one thing to paint for the joy of it, to give herself the chance to paint now and then, as one might give a child a little outing, a visit to the zoo. It was quite another to be asked to be responsible, to be *serious*. "And besides, I'm too old. . . ."

He laughed then, his familiar harsh ironic laugh. "Too old? But not too old to decide that you are the guardian angel of a sick donkey? Too old? But not too old to go around in bright-colored trousers like a gypsy? Too old to be what you have it in you to be? Nonsense!" He was launched now and Joanna watched him erecting his beautiful speech with amused admiration. "What simply baffles me is why you could be so sure that you must bring that animal to Athens, and then tremble before the thing you were obviously really meant to do—paint!" The twinkle had gone from his eye; he had become quite formidable, her frail father whom she had coddled and treated like a child for so long. Joanna felt his power. It was this intelligence, this sensitivity, this hard core in the man which had drawn her mother to him. There under the layers of pretence, under the spoiled child he had let himself become, was the flame, and Joanna recognized it. She would have liked to say then, "The fact is, Papa, that we have each lacked respect for the other." But there is one thing in human life that cannot be changed: no child can take off the mask wholly before a parent.

"Are you listening, Joanna?"

"Oh yes, Papa."

"Well then?"

"I am thinking," Joanna said, quietly. She got up and walked over to the mirror and looked, no longer at him, but straight into her own eyes. What she was out to discover was whether the Joanna who had been able to sit down one morning on Santorini and paint the village for Nicholas could look into her eyes now in Athens, in the apartment, in the presence of her father? She was still not quite sure.

"The thing is," she said turning back, "Papa, I feel as if I had lost a secret. . . ."

"A secret as hard to keep as a donkey in the cellar . . ." he teased.

She stood there, her hands at her sides, as awkward as a child. The recognition, so unexpected and overwhelming, made her feel weak, and in this state of weakness she could not bear his teasing.

"Don't!"

"Don't what?"

"Don't tease me about Ulysses."

"I can't take that donkey very seriously," and he laughed his dry lifeless laugh, more like a cough than a laugh.

It acted like a whip; for just a second Joanna wanted to hit him. And as the silence held, he lifted his eyes, and met the full force of the violence she was withholding. Her silence blazed. And he recognized that fire.

"Don't just stand there . . . looking like your mother!" The words slipped out, but once they had slipped out, there could be no turning back.

"At last!" Joanna breathed.

"At last what?" He shielded his eyes with one hand; he knew very well "what."

"At last you speak to me of her. Papa, Papa!" Good tears streamed down her face like some rich source set free. "Do you realize what these years have been for us? We have been buried here alive!"

"It was too painful . . . I couldn't. . . ."

"Yes, but, oh don't you see? If you shut out pain, you shut out everything, Papa!" Joanna towered there like some leafed-over tree, in a kind of splendor of grief as rich as spring, "Don't you see, how everything stopped— my painting became trivial, my life too. I could not re- member Mother as she was. We shut her out . . . like shutting out life itself!"

The eyes that had looked on her mother with passion- ate love now looked at her as if some locked shutter had opened. They were transparent, as clear as clear blue sea.

"Ulysses is not a joke, Papa! You must understand," and she sat down on the floor at his feet, gentled by his look and kissed her father's hands. "You see, it was as if he broke a spell; I felt myself becoming natural, a human being again . . . I know it sounds absurd."

"A little absurd . . . like Elena." It was the first time in ten years that he had uttered that name.

"On Santorini, she came back to me. Oh Papa, I saw her again as she really was, her hands full of anemones, that day when she was so late for dinner, and you were furious, do you remember?"

"I remember how she died," he said harshly, drawing his hands away. Was it all to begin again?

"No!" Joanna sat back on her knees. She faced him squarely. "Even her death was an act for life. That is what I learned on Santorini . . . a little boy, Nicholas he was called . . . he shone like a star when I told him the story."

"You told a stranger? You could speak of it?"

"Why not? Is it something to be ashamed of? Nicholas made me remember what it is to be a Greek, to rejoice and to be proud! Do we mourn the dead at Thermopylae? No, we rejoice in them. They give us courage!"

"I did not even have the courage to commit suicide," he said quietly. "I just hated myself and the world that went on as if nothing had happened, as if Elena . . ." the words were as bitter as always, but not the hot tears which Joanna felt on her hands as she bent forward to kiss her father. And in her new-found wisdom, she knew that they were healing tears.

"At least we are talking, Papa, talking like two human beings!"

"Rather costly to be human," he said, taking out one of his immaculate white handkerchiefs and blowing his nose. Then he sat back and looked at his daughter with a quite piercing look. "You were such a wild moody little girl, Joanna, but your mother always believed you would be an artist. Hard for a woman to be a real artist, she used to say. Such a woman must have a daemon in her and obey the daemon. One day you came home from school and announced that you were going to be a painter—do you remember?—you must have been about twelve."

"Did I say that? Did I?" Joanna did not remember. How busy she had been all these years trying not to listen to the daemon! "I didn't know then that to be a painter takes time."

"It all takes time," he answered, suddenly brisk, as if after an indulgence in emotion, they were now to deal with practical matters. "But you have come to your senses, through that donkey, or whatever it was. You will give notice tomorrow to those idiots at the office!"

[125

"Oh Papa, I did not know then what faith it would take!"

"Well then," it was his turn to act the avenging angel, "remember your mother and her power to dare! Oh that woman and her daring power!" His laugh now was no longer the dry killing laugh, but came out rich and full. "For her, nothing was impossible. Even to die was not impossible! And that day when she came home so late with the anemones, she made a *mousaka*, do you remember?"

"I remember how she even cooked the way poets write poems, invoking the gods and hoping for the best!"

"So you see, Joanna, what you must do now is to paint seriously in the way your mother made a *mousaka*, as if no one had ever made one before . . . as if the whole world were being re-created by the making of a *mousaka* . . . and she was late as well, you mustn't forget that!"

"But Papa . . ." She was almost convinced.

"Never mind," he answered, for he knew what she was thinking. "We'll take the risk. We may have some hard times. But I have saved, you know, a little. We'll manage, Joanna," he said firmly. "It is going to be all right."

Suddenly Joanna laughed.

"Why are you laughing? I am serious."

"That's just what I used to say to Ulysses when I felt most desperate," she said, "in just that tone of voice, too!"

"How else does one talk to a little donkey?" her father asked, pulling one of her ears as she bent down to kiss the top of his head.

Epilogue

And Ulysses? Joanna herself introduced him to his new life. How splendid he looked in blue beads with bells on his harness, in a flowered hat, his whole back a glory of brilliant hand-woven bags, trotting down to the pier on Mykonos to welcome a boatload of tourists! He proved to be irresistible. They returned that evening in triumph, Joanna whistling, Ulysses stripped of everything except his blue beads, for he had been allowed to eat his hat as a reward for work well done. Even Flavia had to admit that sometimes fantasy and fact become indistinguishable, or, if you will, that hard facts may be turned into miracles when love, imagination, and sheer necessity all work together. If you are sceptical, go to Mykonos and seek out Ulysses!